Love Invents Us

Love, in all its inconvenient and unacceptable forms – desperately longed-for or unbidden, coming at the wrong time or for the wrong person – is both the despair and the saving grace of the people in Amy Bloom's wonderfully rich novel.

Elizabeth Taube, shy, chubby, unmoored, with parents as remote as planets, has to take love where she finds it: at the sweet counter in Frank's Five and Dime; in the dusty treasures revealed to her by Mrs Hill, the elderly black woman she visits (and steals from); in the mirror at Furs by Klein, where Mr Klein lets her try on his coats; and in the admiring, helpless gaze of Max Stone, her married English teacher. She takes love in all these places, watching for clues to who she might be, trying on selves for their admiring eyes.

And then, as she watches her high school basketball team practice one day, love takes her completely in the person of Huddie Lester. Huddie's life, like Max's, is taken over by his love for Elizabeth. They are captured from the moment he puts his hand beside her leg on the bench in the high school gym, so close that they both feel the soft prickling of tiny hairs on her thigh. Love takes Elizabeth, Huddie and the others whose lives intertwine with theirs in this intricate and many-layered novel, into places they never expected to be, and unknown parts of themselves.

Amy Bloom's stunningly perspicacious, jewel-like prose perfectly captures the bittersweet process by which we come to know that though love may not heal or save us or hand us a happy ending, in the end it invents us all.

Also by Amy Bloom in Picador
COME TO ME

Love
Invents Us

Amy Bloom

PICADOR

First published 1997 by Random House Inc., New York
and simultaneously in Canada by Random House of Canada Limited, Toronto

First published in Great Britain 1997 by Picador

an imprint of Macmillan Publishers Ltd
25 Eccleston Place, London SW1W 9NF
and Basingstoke

Associated companies throughout the world

ISBN 0 330 35068 4

1 3 5 7 9 8 6 4 2

A CIP catalogue record for this book is available from
the British Library.

Printed and bound in Great Britain by
Mackays of Chatham plc, Chatham, Kent

FOR ALEXANDER, CAITLIN, AND SARAH

. . . there are many ways to be born and
They all come forth, in their own grace.
—Muriel Rukeyser

. . . the great and incalculable grace of love, which says, with Augustine, "I want you to be," without being able to give any particular reason for such supreme and unsurpassable affirmation.

—Hannah Arendt

PART I

JUST AS I AM

▼

I wasn't surprised to find myself in the back of Mr. Klein's store, wearing only my undershirt and panties, surrounded by sable.

"Sable is right for you, Lizbet," Mr. Klein said, draping a shawl-collared jacket over me. "Perfect for your skin and your eyes. A million times a day the boys must tell you. Such skin."

No one except Mr. Klein had ever suggested that my appearance was pleasing. My mother took time out from filling half the houses on Long Island with large French cachepots and small porcelain dogs to take me shopping at Lord and Taylor's Pretty Plus; her aesthetic sense made her look the other way when the saleswomen dragged me out in navy blue A-line dresses and plaid jumpers. Looking at me sideways, she saw the chewed ends of my hair, smudged pink harlequin glasses, a bad attitude.

I stood on a little velvet footstool and modeled fur coats for Mr. Klein. He had suggested I take off my perpetual green corduroys and hooded sweatshirt so we could see how the coats really looked. I agreed, only pretending to hesitate for a minute so I could watch his thin grey face expand and pinken.

I felt the warm rushing in my chest that being with him gave me. He also gave me Belgian chocolate, because he felt Hershey's wasn't good enough for me, and he told me that if only God had blessed him and Mrs. Klein with a wonderful daughter like me, he would be truly happy, *kayn ahora*. My mother never said I was wonderful. My father, whose admiration for my mother had diminished only a little over the years, was certainly not heard thanking God for giving him the gift of me.

"This one next, Lizbet." Mr. Klein handed me a small mink coat and set a mink beret on my dirty hair.

"This is my size. Do kids wear mink coats?"

If you had to dress up, mink was the way to go. Much better than my scratchy navy wool, designed to turn chubby Jewish girls into pale Victorian wards. The fur brushed my chin, and without my glasses (Mr. Klein and I agreed that it was a shame to hide my lovely eyes and so we put my glasses in his coat pocket during our modeling sessions) I felt glamorously Russian. I couldn't see a thing. He put the beret at a slight angle and stepped back, admiring me in my bare feet and my mink.

"Perfect. This is how a fur coat should look on a girl. Not some little stick girl in rabbit. This is an ensemble."

I turned around to see what I could of myself from the back: a brown triangle topped by a white blur and another brown smudge.

I modeled two more coats, a ranch mink, which displeased Mr. Klein with its careless stitching, and a fox cape, which made us both smile. Even Mr. Klein thought floor-length silver fox was a little much.

As always, he turned his back as I pulled on my jeans and sweatshirt. I sat down on one of the spindly pink velvet chairs, putting my sneakers on as he put away the coats.

We said nothing on the drive home. I ate my chocolate and Mr. Klein turned on WQXR, the only time I ever listened to classical music. Mr. Klein rounded my driveway, trying to look unconcerned. I think we both expected that one Monday my parents would finally come rushing out of the house, appalled and avenging.

I went inside, my shoelaces flapping against the hallway's glazed, uneven brick. Could anything be less inviting than a brick foyer? It pressed into the soles of my feet, and every dropped and delicate object shattered irretrievably.

I know some cleaning lady greeted me; we alternated between elderly Irish women, who looked as though they'd been born to rid the world of lazy people's private filth, and middle-aged Bolivian women quietly stalking dust and our greasy, oversized fingerprints.

Every dinner was a short horror; my eating habits were remarked upon, and then my mother would talk about politics and decorating and my wardrobe. My father talked about his clients, their divorces, their bank accounts. I would go to my room, pretend to do my homework, and read my novels. In my room, I was the Scarlet Pimpernel. Sometimes I was Sydney Carton and once in a while I was Tarzan. I went to sleep dreaming of the nineteenth century, my oldest, largest teddy bear held tightly between my legs.

Mr. Klein usually drove up beside me as I was walking to the bus stop. When I saw the tip of his huge, unfashionable blue Cadillac slowly slide by me and pause, I skipped ahead and dropped my books on the front seat, spared another day of riding the school bus. He dropped me off in front of Arrandale Elementary School as the buses discharged all the kids I had managed to avoid thus far.

On the mornings Mr. Klein failed to appear, I kept a low profile and worried about him until the routine of school settled upon me. I was vulnerable again only at recess. The first two days of kindergarten had taught me to carry a book everywhere, and as soon as I found a place on the pebbled asphalt, I had only to set my eyes on the clean black letters and the soft ivory page and I would be gone, spirited right out of what passed for my real life.

Our first trip to Furs by Klein was incidental, barely a foreshadowing of our afternoons together. Mr. Klein passed me on the way home from school. Having lost two notebooks since school began, I'd missed the bus while searching the halls frantically for my third—bright red canvas designed to be easily seen. I started home, a couple of miles through the sticky, smoky leaf piles and across endless emerald lawns. No one knew I liked to walk. Mr. Klein pulled up ahead of me and signaled, shyly. I ran to the car, gratified to tears by a smile I could see from the road.

"I'll give you a ride home, but I need to stop back at my shop, something I forgot. All right?"

I nodded. It was better than all right. Maybe I'd never have to go home. He could drive me to Mexico, night after night through the Great Plains, and I wouldn't mind.

Furs by Klein stood on the corner of Shore Drive, its curved, pink-tinted windows and black lacquered French doors the height of suburban elegance. Inside stood headless

bodies, six rose-velvet torsos, each wearing a fur coat. There
were mirrors everywhere I looked and a few thin-legged, arm-
less chairs. The walls were lined with coats and jackets and
capes. Above them, floating on transparent necks, were the
hats.

Mr. Klein watched me. "Go ahead," he said. "All ladies like
hats." He pulled down a few and walked discreetly into the
workroom at the rear. I tried on a black cloche with a dotted
veil and then a kelly-green fedora with a band of arching
brown feathers. Mr. Klein emerged from the back, his hands
in the pockets of his baggy grey trousers.

"Come, Lizbet, your mother will be worried about you.
Leave the hats, It's all right. Mondays are the day off, the girls
will put them back tomorrow." He turned out the lights and
opened the door for me.

"My mother's not home." I'm really an orphan, adopt me.

"Tcha, I am so absentminded. Mrs. Klein tells me your
mother is a famous decorator. Of course she is out—decorating."

He smiled, just slightly, and I laughed out loud. He's on my
side.

Almost every morning now, he gave me a ride to school.
Without any negotiating that I remember, I knew that on
Monday afternoons I would miss my bus and he would pick
me up as I walked down Arrandale Avenue. I would keep him
company while he did whatever he did in the back room and
I tried on hats. After a few Mondays I eyed the coats.

"Of course," he said. "When you're grown up, you'll tell
your husband, 'Get me a sable from Klein's. It's Klein's or
nothing.' " He waggled a finger sternly, showing me who I

would be: a pretty young woman with a rich, indulgent husband. "Let me help you."

Mr. Klein slipped an ash-blonde mink jacket over my sweatshirt and admired me aloud. Soon after, he stopped going into the workroom, and soon after that, I began taking off my clothes. The pleasure on Mr. Klein's face made me forget everything I heard in the low tones of my parents' conversation and everything I saw in my own mirror. I chose to believe Mr. Klein.

At home, to conjure up the feeling of Mr. Klein's cool round fingertips on my shoulders, touching me lightly before the satin lining descended, I listened to classical music. My father made approving snorts behind *The Wall Street Journal.*

I lay on the floor of the living room, behind the biggest couch, and saw myself playing the piano, adult and beautifully formed. I am wearing a dress I saw on Marilyn Monroe, the sheerest clinging net, with sparkling stones coming up over the tips of my breasts and down between my legs. I am moving slowly across the stage, the wide hem of my sable cape shaping a series of round, dark waves. I hand the cape to an adoring Mr. Klein, slightly improved and handsomely turned out in a tuxedo cut just like my father's.

My mother stepped over me and then stopped. I was eye to toe with her tiny pink suede loafers and happy to stay that way. Her round blue eyes and her fear of wrinkles made her stare as harsh and haunting as the eyeless Greek heads she'd put in my father's study.

"Keeping busy, are you, Elizabeth?"

I couldn't imagine what prompted this. My mother usually acted as though I had been raised by a responsible, affectionate governess; guilt and love were as foreign to her as butter and sugar.

"Yeah. School, books." I studied the little gold bar across the tongue of her right loafer.

"And all is well?"

"Fine. Everything's fine."

"You wouldn't like to study an instrument, would you? Piano? Perhaps a piano in the library. That could be attractive. An older piece, deep browns, a maroon paisley shawl, silver picture frames. Quite attractive."

"I don't know. Can I think about it?" I didn't mind being part of my mother's endless redecorating; in the past, her domestic fantasies had produced my queen-size brass bed, which I loved, and a giant Tudor dollhouse, complete with chiming doorbell and working shower.

"Of course, think it over. Let's make a decision next week, shall we?" She started to touch my hair and patted me on the shoulder instead.

I didn't see Mr. Klein until the following Monday. I endured four mornings at the bus stop: leaves stuffed down my shirt, books knocked into the trash can, lunch bag tossed from boy to boy. Fortunately, the bus driver was a madman, and his rageful mutterings and yelping at invisible assailants captured whatever attention might have come my way once we were on the bus.

It was raining that Monday, and I wondered if I should walk anyway. I never thought about the fact that Mr. Klein and I had no way to contact each other. I could only wait, in silence. I pulled up my hood and started walking down Arrandale, waiting for a blue streak to come past my left side, waiting for the slight skid of wet leaves as Mr. Klein braked to a stop. Finally, much closer to home than usual, the car came.

"You're almost home," he said. "Maybe I should just take you home? We can go to the store another time." He looked rushed and unhappy.

"Sure, if you don't have time, that's okay."

"I have the time, *tsatskela*. I have the time." He turned the car around and drove us back to Furs by Klein.

I got out and waited in the rain while he unlocked the big black doors.

"You're soaking wet," he said harshly. "You should have taken the bus."

"I missed it," I lied. If he wasn't going to admit that he wanted me to miss the bus, I wasn't going to admit that I had missed it for him.

"Yes, you miss the bus, I pick you up. Lizbet, you are a very special girl, and standing around an old man's shop in wet clothes is not what you should be doing."

What I usually did was stand around in no clothes at all, but I could tell that Mr. Klein, like most adults, was now working only from his version of the script.

I sat down uneasily at the little table with the swiveling gilt-framed mirror, ready to try on hats. Without Mr. Klein's encouragement, I wouldn't even look at the coats. He didn't hand me any hats.

He pressed his thin sharp face deep into the side of my neck, pushing my sweatshirt aside with one hand. I looked in the mirror and saw my own round wet face, comic in its surprise and pink glasses. I saw Mr. Klein's curly grey hair and a bald spot I would have never discovered otherwise.

"Get your coat." He rubbed his face with both hands and stood by the door.

"I don't have a coat."

"They let you go in the rain, with no coat? *Gottenyu*. Let's go, please." He held the door open for me and I had to walk through it.

The chocolate wasn't my usual Belgian slab. It was a deep gold-foil box tied with pink and gold wisps, and topped with a cluster of sparkling gold berries. He dropped it in my lap like something diseased.

I held on to the box, stroking the fairy ribbons, until he told me to open it.

Each of the six chocolates had a figure on top. Three milk, three bittersweet, each one carved with angel wings or a heart or a white-rimmed rose. In our fat-free home, my eating habits were regarded as criminal. My parents would no more have bought me beautiful chocolates than gift-wrapped a gun for a killer.

"Lizbet . . ."

He looked out the window at the rain and I looked up at him quickly. I had obviously done something wrong, and although my parents' anger and chagrin didn't bother me a bit, his unhappiness was pulling me apart. I crushed one of the chocolates with my fingers, and Mr. Klein saw me.

"Nah, nah," he said softly, wiping my fingers with his handkerchief. He cleared his throat. "My schedule's changing. I won't be able to give you rides after school. I'm going to open the shop on Mondays."

"How about in the morning?" I didn't know I could talk through this kind of pain.

"I don't think so. I need to get in a little earlier. It's not so bad, you should ride with other boys and girls. You'll see, you'll have a good time."

I sat there sullenly, ostentatiously mashing the chocolates.

"Too bad, they're very nice chocolates. Teuscher's. Remember, sable from Klein's, chocolate from Teuscher's. Only the best for you. I'm telling you, only the best."

"I'm not going to have a good time on the bus." I didn't mash the last chocolate, I just ran a fingertip over the tiny ridges of the rosebud.

"Maybe not. I shouldn't have said you'd have a good time. I'm sorry." He sighed and looked away.

I bit into the last chocolate. "Here, you have some too."

"No, they're for you. They were all for you."

"I'm not that hungry. Here." I held out the chocolate half, and he lowered his head, startling me. I put my fingers up to his narrow lips, and he took the chocolate neatly between his teeth. I could feel the very edge of his teeth against my fingers.

We pulled up in front of my house, and he put his hand over mine, for just one moment.

"I'll say it again, only the best is good enough for you. So, we'll say au revoir, Lizbet. Elizabeth. Not good-bye."

"Au revoir. Thank you very much for the chocolates." My mother's instructions surfaced at odd times.

I left my dripping sneakers on the brick floor, dropped my wet clothes into my lilac straw hamper, and took my very first voluntary shower. I dried off slowly, watching myself in the steamy mirror. When I didn't come down for dinner, my mother found me, naked and quiet, deep in my covers.

"Let's get the piano," I said.

I started lessons with Mr. Canetti the next week. He served me wine-flavored cookies instead of chocolate. One day he bent forward to push my sleeves back over my aching wrists, and I saw my beautiful self take shape in his eyes. I loved him, too.

TAKE MY HAND

▼

I found comfort in the red, shy eyes of Mr. Klein and Mr. Canetti, and I found it in Frank's Five and Dime. I didn't think of it as stealing; I didn't brag about it to other kids, not that I talked to them anyway, and I didn't pray for forgiveness. It was just Taking. Every school day I took Necco wafers and a Heath bar from Frank's. It was a long, dim box of a room; the candy racks were in front of the cash register, halfway down the left wall facing a heavy glass case, five shelves filled with Madame Alexander dolls and their hats and shoes and luggage sets. I walked in ten minutes before school started most days and cruised the shop, pausing in front of the doll case, looking for the little knot of businessmen and newspapers to stand behind. I was a terrible thief, slow and sticky and predictable. Without my round, trusting face and geeky glasses, I would never have gotten as far as I did. I put the Neccos, shifting in their glassy opaque tube, into my lunch bag and held the Heath bar in my coat pocket. It was easily unwrapped, one blind finger sliding under the smooth brown back flap. Once, my pocket lining was torn and I had to tuck it in the waistband of my panties and get it out during coatroom time. I smelled of anxious sweat and chocolate all day.

I got caught. Frank wrapped his huge hand around my wrist and squeezed until I dropped my lunch bag on the counter. He took out the candy, and I said, my mind blank with humiliation, that I had intended to pay for it.

"Sure you did. Every day you come in here. For this. Get outta here and don't come back."

Ellyn and Cindi Kramer stood in the doorway, listening openmouthed, and looked at me with real pleasure as I walked between them. It could have been worse; he could have telephoned my parents, who surely would have made me go to the psychiatrist I'd been ducking for the last year. I didn't want to talk about what I did and why; I already knew I was crazy. As it was, I entered hell all by myself, like everyone else.

What I did at Mrs. Hill's wasn't stealing, either. Stealing was sneaking lipstick from Woolworth's or blue silk panties from Bee's Lingerie Shop. After Frank's, after months of being called a thief by the whole bus, every single day, of being followed down the street by Ellyn and Cindi, catcalling until I reached the hedges that marked our property, I stayed out of candy stores, but I still stole. By the middle of seventh grade, I was casually lining up pens, fluorescent markers, and leather barrettes on one long table in study hall like it was the local flea market. But everything I took from Mrs. Hill I hid in my closet. Every time the doorbell rang I could see two big cops, hands on their guns, standing in my mother's foyer and calling out my name.

Mrs. Hill was almost blind, she had something-retinitis; there was a hole in the center of her vision, as if someone had ripped the middle out of every page. If she turned her head way to the right or left, she could just about see my face. When I walked toward her as she sat in the big red vinyl recliner, she would turn her face far to the right; the closer I got, the more she would seem to yearn toward the kitchen. When I was almost upon her, she would smile away from me.

Every Saturday I tidied up Mrs. Hill's house and made her lunch and dinner. She was my good deed, courtesy of Samuel C. Shales, minister at the Beech Street A.M.E. Zion Church, Where Everybody Is Somebody and Jesus Is Lord Over All. At eleven o'clock on September 16, through the window of my algebra class, I heard gospel music for the first time. Those sweet, meaty sounds led me to a white wood church on a corner my school bus never passed. Each time I had to walk by Reverend Shales' office, and each time he looked up and kept talking on the phone. I stayed near the church bulletin board, my eyes down, my heart singing like Mahalia Jackson.

Reverend Shales was shorter than I'd thought, and his glasses shimmered in the dusty light.

"Miss? You're visiting our church again?"

I said yes. He asked my name, my parents' names, my address, and my school, and however embarrassed I was to be caught lurking in his church hall, he was not sorry to have me there. His eyes shone like black pearls. I seemed like a girl who could offer a little companionship, he said. I could run to the corner store and bring back the right change, couldn't I? I wasn't above a little light cleaning, was I? He invited me to come and listen to the choir whenever I liked, and at the same time take the opportunity, the special opportunity to serve, to offer Christian charity to a very sweet, very lovely elderly lady a few doors down. He led me out the church door and pointed down the street to the small white house with the patchy lawn and the listing porch.

"I'll phone Miz Hill to say you're on your way. You are on your way now, young lady." And he put his big hand on the small of my back and pushed. He said Go, and I went.

Crinkly, lifeless grey curls floated up and across Mrs. Hill's grey-brown scalp, winging out over her ears. What must have been round, brown eyes had become opaque beige slits, like two additional spots of smooth skin in her dark puckered face. She had seven housedresses, and her doctor daughter came home twice a year from the great, safe distance of California and replaced them all. Mrs. Hill did not rotate them as Dr. Hill intended; she wore the pink one all week, and when it was stiff with sweat and moisturizer and medicated cream for her eczema, she threw it in the hamper for me to wash. On Saturdays she wore the purple housedress, and I didn't blame her a bit. It was the least practical of them; instead of a cotton-poly mix, it was soft velour, and the pull on the end of the zipper was a purple and yellow sunflower, as though van Gogh had gotten loose in the Sears catalog. In her purple sunflower robe, Mrs. Hill told my fortune.

"Long life here," she said, one thick, twisted finger digging into the middle of my palm. "Love affairs here. Did you bring Mrs. Hill some pork rinds?"

Dr. Hill had sent a note that Mrs. Hill had all sorts of things wrong with her heart and that salt and fat were out of the question. Mrs. Hill and I had a deal: one palm reading for a bag of Salty Jim's Pork Rinds. Mrs. Hill told me that Salty Jim was really Jim Buckton, who played trumpet with Duke Ellington in the fifties and had gone to high school with Mrs. Hill. Out of respect and school loyalty, we usually ate Salty Jim's, but when the Red Owl Supermarket carried Li'l Pig Bar-B-Que Pork Rinds, we had to give old Jim the heave-ho and stock up on orange-speckled, amber clouds of pork fat.

"Open up that bag and set it right here. Let's have that hand." I popped open two cans of grape soda.

Mrs. Hill bent over my palm, and I could smell the greasy fruit smell of her hair pomade and the piercing eucalyptus of Vicks VapoRub, which she used prophylactically.

"The love affairs startin' early." She jabbed my palm and then held my own hand up to me, showing me the point at which the love line joined the life line.

"Really?" I said. I didn't think of Mr. Klein or Mr. Canetti as love affairs. I knew that they had loved me and I had loved them back, but there wasn't any sex, and you couldn't have an affair without sex. When I was in fifth grade I had had a little sex with Seth Stern, but it wasn't what I thought a love affair should be. We were playing James Bond, and he pulled down my underpants and stuck his hand between my legs. He was only in sixth grade, but he was shaving already, and I found the red nicks on his throat and chin mysterious, alluring tribal scars. He stuck one long finger inside me and rocked me roughly on his hand until we heard our parents gathering coats in the front hall. He pushed me back onto the bed and yanked up my panties while running his thumb along the inside of my thigh. My parents called for me, and we went downstairs, all my attention on my bruised, wet center and on Seth, who insisted on shaking my father's hand as we said good-bye. The tension and excitement and shame I felt were terrible and vivid. This was *life*. Out of remorse, or indifference, he wouldn't answer my phone calls, and my parents had just about dropped the Sterns anyway, so I kept my virginity quite a while longer. I dreamt of his hands.

Mrs. Hill leaned back in her recliner and twisted her face away to watch me.

"In my closet there's a hatbox, an old red hatbox. Bring it to me, sugar."

Mrs. Hill only used endearments when she was asking me a favor or criticizing me.

The closet would have been my mother's worst nightmare: blouses lying on the floor in their own wrinkled, dusty puddles, single shoes turned heel up, sticking into piles of sweaters and pants. On the top shelf were three hatboxes, one faded red, one with green and white stripes, and a yellowed one with grimy ivory tassels hanging from the sides. Mrs. Hill was much shorter than I was and could barely hobble from room to room; the hatboxes and the shelf they sat on were covered in dust.

Mrs. Hill rested the red hatbox in her purple velour lap, her bony knees hunched up to keep it from sliding to the floor. "Some pretty things in here. If I kept them out, a burglar might get them. No burglar's going hunting through an old lady's underthings, through a messy old closet." I was always looking to justify the mess in my room, too.

Mrs. Hill lifted off the lid and handed it to me, the thick dust rippling slightly.

"What about these, miss? You don't see these anymore."

They were eight long silver straws with filigreed hearts at their ends. Mrs. Hill handed them to me one by one, and I ran my fingers over the thin silver lacework around the hearts' edges. She waved one straw in the air.

"Spoons for iced tea. Plus the stems are hollow, so you can sip too. Wedding present." She closed her eyes. "Wedding present from Alva and Edna Thomas, he worked with Mr. Hill. Iced tea and strawberry shortcake in the summer. And brandy cup and lemon cake with burnt sugar frosting at Christmas."

I had never seen anything so fancy and frivolous in all my life. My parents' house was all handsome, angular teak and tautly rounded leather, and each decorative piece had the added weight of culture or art or good taste. These were just pretty and gay, and as I held them I could feel that if I pressed down any harder at all, the hollow stems would give way.

"Are you going to give them to your daughter?" I asked, sure that the Dr. Vivian Hill in the pastel-tinted eight-by-ten on the mantelpiece, with one manicured hand on the hood of a big white Mercedes, black eyes flatly daring us to wonder how she got from here to there, would not want the spoons, or anything else from this small house with the rutted floors and soiled lampshades. Dr. Hill's old bedroom was now the storage room—wire hangers, dresses from twenty years ago, shoes slit for corns and bunions and still not right, cat food for the cat that died six months before I came, cookie tins filled with rubber bands and green stamps. The only bit of Dr. Hill left was the graduation tassel used to pull down the window shade. Dr. Hill stayed at the Great Neck Inn when she visited.

Mrs. Hill made a feeble grab for the spoons, snatching at the air to my left. "Give them to Vivian? Why should I give them to anyone? I'm not dead. Gimme those spoons, girl."

I put all but one of the spoons back into her hands; they stuck out like silver pins in an old brown cushion. She sorted them and wrapped them in the tissue paper. Before she could count them up and accuse me, I handed her the last one.

"Don't forget this, it fell off your lap," I lied.

She gestured for the lid. "Next time, we can look at some more treasures," she said.

I put the red hatbox back and quickly lifted out the striped one. Inside were twelve silver spoons with short, thickly twisted stems, the ends crowned with tiny enameled portraits of long-haired, biblical-looking men. Each little white face was touched with two pink dots for cheeks and pairs of blue or brown dots for eyes. Their hair was several different shades of brown.

"Don't be goin' in my things, now."

"I'm not, I was just trying to get this put back where it belongs. I was tidying up your closet, as a matter of fact."

"Uh-huh. Snooping and spying is more like it."

I knew she didn't mind; it wasn't like there were millions of people interested in Mrs. Hill's life, never mind the contents of her closet.

Mrs. Hill had two cookbooks: *The Joy of Cooking* and *The Paschal Lamb,* which was put out by the Greater A.M.E. Zion

Church of Philadelphia and was almost as long as the gravy-stained Rombauer bible. I read them both, and once Mrs. Hill showed me how to light her chipped gas stove, I was fearless. I didn't see what harm I could do. No Limoges plates to break, nothing to stain or put back the wrong way, no system to throw out of whack. Mrs. Hill's spice rack was six tins of Durkee's in a shoebox on the counter. I put my hair in a ponytail, and Mrs. Hill wrapped a pink gingham towel around my waist. I made chicken-and-dumplings. I used lard and corn-flake crumbs, and when Mrs. Hill said she'd loved Brunswick stew as a girl, I turned to page 88 in the *Lamb* and said, "All I need is corn. And a squirrel." I made sweet potato casserole and angels on horseback for Mrs. Hill's birthday. I made lasagna and divided it into four little loaf pans so Mrs. Hill could just heat them up during the week. I precooked them so if she didn't have the energy to put them in the oven she could eat them cold without getting some kind of uncooked-meat disease.

At school on Monday, I asked Mimi Tedeschi, who practically lived in church, who she thought the men on the spoons could be.

"The apostles. Don't you know who the apostles are? Peter, Andrew, John, Matthias, James the Greater . . ." She rattled off all twelve names. "I guess being Jewish you didn't learn about them. My grandmother has a set like that. Apostle spoons. Hers are all on a little wood stand over the fireplace."

After a few Saturdays, Mrs. Hill and I had gone through all three hatboxes. Besides the apostles and the iced tea stirrers, there were two small bowls of cranberry glass set in baskets of braided gold wire; four monogrammed silver napkin rings; six half-size teacups and matching saucers, each with a different flower garlanding the sides of the cup and the face of the saucer, each with one coy bud resting at the bottom of the cup. I loved them all. Mrs. Hill would hand them to me to admire, and then we'd rewrap them in tissue and I'd put them back in the closet.

In November, Mrs. Hill was always cold. She was tired of the hatboxes, tired of reading my palm, and tired of lasagna. She would fall asleep around two and wake up as the sky was getting dark.

"Don't you leave while I'm sleeping. Elizabeth, you hear me? Don't you leave if I'm not awake."

"Okay. I mean, even if I did, you'd be fine. I mean, nothing would happen."

"Don't tell me what's gonna happen in my own house. You come and wake me up before you leave."

"Yes, ma'am."

The next Saturday, she fell asleep in her chair right after lunch. I went into her bedroom and stood in the mouth of the closet, staring up at the row of hatboxes. I took down the apostles and chose one whose eyes seemed to tilt up at me beneath lashes as dark and spiky as Seth Stern's. I put him into my backpack and changed Mrs. Hill's bed, trying to hold my breath until I got the clean sheets on and the old ones stuffed into the washer.

The following Saturday, I took one with blue eyes, and the Saturday after that, another dark-eyed one. I wanted to take the lady's-slipper teacup next.

Mrs. Hill said to me, "Could you come this Tuesday? Vivian's coming by, for just a little while. I think we could do a little cleaning up before."

I had to smile; when "we" cleaned up, Mrs. Hill put on an old plaid apron and sat back in her recliner while I scrubbed the backsplash and threw out dead plants and moldy bread.

I didn't like cleaning, and Mrs. Hill never offered to pay me, and even if she had, Reverend Shales had made it very clear that I was not ever to take money from her.

"I can't. I've got school stuff. The paper. I have to go to a meeting." I didn't think Mrs. Hill would know that the special ed class put out the school paper all by itself.

"I think you might have to skip that meeting, sugar. I don't like to put you out, you know that, but I really do need your help on Tuesday. Can't have my Doctor FancyPants shakin' her head, talkin' about putting Mrs. Hill in some *home*. I need you Tuesday."

If I came Tuesday, I would be there all the time. I could feel her need for me reaching out like terrible black roots, wrapping themselves right around me, burying me in wet brown earth.

"I'm really sorry. I just can't. I have to be at that meeting. Maybe there's someone else from church." The A.M.E. Zion Church seemed to me to be overflowing with neatly dressed gloved and hatted ladies eager to help.

"Have someone from church come in here? Don't talk crazy. You're the one I need. And I need you on Tuesday. It's not too much to ask if you think on it."

I didn't say anything, hoping that she'd get embarrassed about being so insistent.

"Come here, sugar. It's not too much to ask since you've got three of my spoons. Three silver spoons and you won't come on Tuesday and help out your friend Mrs. Hill? I call that selfish. And stupid. I call that stupid. Steal from me and then make me mad? Don't you think I'm going to go right to Reverend Shales and tell him that nice little Jewish girl he found for me is stealing my silver? Don't you think I'm going to have to call your father and tell him that his daughter's a thief, taking advantage of a poor old lady, half-blind and living all on her own?"

"Jesus," I said, keeping my voice low, so she wouldn't leap out of her recliner and attack me.

"Don't *you* call on Jesus." Her voice softened. "You can have the spoons. You can have a teacup too. I can't get by with only Saturdays, and that's the truth." She leaned back in her chair, pressing her cheek into the ratty old doily she'd pinned to the headrest.

I went over to her, more ashamed that I had made her beg than about the stealing. I would make it up to her; I would walk in the pathways of righteousness every Tuesday, Thursday, and Saturday for the rest of her life.

A BALM IN GILEAD

▼

Ellyn and Cindi, who had followed me faithfully every day through the winter of sixth grade yelling "Thou shalt not steal" and "Watch your stuff, here comes the thief," moved on to boys and pretty, popular, less honestly aggressive selves. They said hi when we passed in the halls, to show that they were *nice* girls, but they didn't say my name, to make it clear that I was not part of their group. There was only one person still interested in my criminal past, a big redheaded eighth-grader, arms like pocked marble, lashless blue frog eyes watching for me as she leaned, surefooted and excited, on the door of my locker. I was so far off the mainland of junior high that I couldn't see she was barely one notch above me on the reject pile. I didn't even know she was crazy, but I don't think anyone did. I thought she was just mean and my destiny.

I tried to find safe corner seats at isolated tables for study hall, but every other day Deenie sat down across from me. The first Monday, she cracked her knuckles a few times and handed me a sheet of paper. She had drawn a picture of a fat little girl hanging from a gibbet, wavy lines indicating the swinging of her feet. In later pictures the girl was frying in the electric chair, hair sprayed straight out from her head; one time she was lying in six pieces on the ground, with "Thief = Shit" carefully blocked out under her in strawberry-scented marker. Deenie smiled at me, clinically curious. I counted the dots in the grey ceiling tiles, wondering whether I would die or just be paralyzed for life if I jumped from the second-story window. I bit the insides of my cheeks to keep my face still and ran my tongue over the tiny grooved holes inside my mouth. Her notes got more elaborate, whole paragraphs describing my crimes, illustrated by drawings of my violent, Road Runner–like deaths. At the end of seventh grade she went to a private high school. Five years later, I saw her sitting across from me at the Aegean Diner, drinking coffee and poking at piles of change scattered over the tabletop. Her red hair was dyed black. She nodded vaguely, and I have to say I was a little hurt that she didn't remember me.

Eighth grade. Mr. O'Donnell discovered that I had the uncanny and otherwise useless gift of flawless sentence diagramming. If I was allowed to leave class and go to the lunchroom, I brought back twenty-eight perfectly corrected papers. I didn't have to take a single English test that year, and got on good terms with the cafeteria ladies, who used to fold their arms in front of the baked goods when they saw me coming. Now we were all pals. I walked in three times a week with a quarter for the carton of milk for Mr. O'Donnell's ulcer, a fat sheaf of papers under my arm, and my new Saint Christopher medal around my neck. I'd found it in the girls' room and thought that if anyone should have one, it was me. It looked good down between my breasts, knocking against the pink bow on my bra.

There were other, fatter girls in navy blue A-line skirts and loose sweaters, arranging and rearranging the Honor Society bake sale table, running their fingers along plate edges and cupcake overhangs, and other, braver girls in sloppy shirts and overalls, their long hair twisted up in barrettes they'd made at Buck's Rock leather shop, sitting on the back stairs passing cigarettes around. I clung to my own marginal, frightened identity and refused to be part of any group that would have me.

My mother went to England for two weeks in October, and my father went to Oregon after Thanksgiving. She brought me a white cashmere cardigan and he brought me a malachite butterfly on a silver chain and I thought both were pretty in their way and I lost them. I don't remember anything else about eighth grade because my body took over my life. The changes surprised me, even though I'd seen the Snow White and Her Menstrual Cycle filmstrip in sixth grade. Everything was moving, even while I slept, and when I woke up, flesh I had known my whole life had slid off or moved down or hidden itself under a blanket of thin dark hair. I wouldn't have mentioned my period to my mother at all if I hadn't had to apologize for the blood smeared across the top and bottom sheets, seeping down to cling to the ruffled edges of my lilac shorty pajamas. My mother stripped my bed herself and plunged everything into cold water in the tub as I stood behind her in my wet pajamas, pressing my legs together to keep blood from dripping onto the lilac bath mat. Right then, chin tucked down to steady the pile of clean linen, she was not my chill, familiar mother. She was the woman in overalls who attacked white fly in the greenhouse, who rubbed an ice cube against a wad of bubblegum stuck in my hair down to the scalp, and took it out without a cross word. Her suddenly rough, competent hands snapped in the pleasure of the task, and her lips set in a cheerful can-do line. I longed for her the way lovers in movies longed for each other, across time and space, their eyes looking right past what was possible.

She pushed me down on the toilet seat with one tiny hand. I waited for her to come back, afraid to move until she brought me what I knew would be the right thing; she came in with a small blue box of Tampax and a pair of dry underpants.

"Don't wear light colors when you have it, lovey," she said, and left, and I pressed my face against the clean pajamas.

My mother had rules and guidelines for life, and although none of them applied to the life I'd led so far, she delivered them with great force, sometimes digging her hand into my shoulder until I nodded. Only beauty gives life meaning, she said. Good manners are more important, and more durable, than feelings. Natural fibers and a flattering cut are all that matter in clothing. Also, men do not know what they do not know, and women should not tell them. These ideas were held by my mother's friends, too: "progressive," apparently romantic, sixth-generation upper-class daughters of twits and earls. Everyone who knew our family knew that my mother was the daughter of a barrister and his landed-gentry wife, both tragically killed in the Blitz; in some stories they were buried in each other's arms, in my favorite they were overcome by smoke after pulling their servants out of the burning rubble.

What everyone knew was a lie, except the English part. My mother was the illegitimate daughter of a London prostitute who had just enough feeling for her newborn baby to bundle her up in a stained sheet and deliver her, clots of blood still clinging to her little scalp, to Great-aunt Lil in Putney. My mother left school and Putney (and Aunt Lil and Cousin Harriet) at sixteen. World War Two gave her the opportunity to re-create herself. She took off for Liverpool and ran goods for black-marketeers and did other things that the poor and resourceful do in major ports.

When I read *The Little Princess* I saw my mother, not myself, as the forlorn, aristocratic little girl, befriended and heaped with presents by the very kind and very rich Indian Gentleman. I identified with her starving, dim-witted companion, roll crammed into her mouth, eyes darting in terror as she muttered thanks in dreadful yowling tones. If I had met the brave, lying girl Cousin Harriet knew, I think I would have liked her. I could have admired her improvised and perfected self; the pinched, pasty face turned into fashionable slenderness, terrible abandonment replayed as well-bred self-sufficiency. We both knew I was not the daughter she'd planned for, was not at all the necessary, dimpled denial of Aunt Lil's boardinghouse, of night bicycle rides, two pints of gin strapped under her jacket, butter sweating through waxed paper in her book bag; of head lice and chopped-off hair. Cousin Harriet visited when I was eight and spent our only weekend together setting my straight hair on hot metal rollers until my scalp blistered and telling me the truth about my mother. As she unrolled one stiff, stupid ringlet after another, I saw the nuns sweeping my mother's blonde curls across the room and into the dustbin and my mother turning her back to the class.

"No blubbing, mind you, like the other little girls, just wet eyes. And only cried a bit when we walked home."

Margaret was brought to the States by Stan Muslic, an army captain, who married her somewhere near the family's dairy farm in Ithaca. (Cousin Harriet was not sure about Ithaca, but was very sure about the farm part.) For all I know, she loved Captain Muslic madly, and his absurd death, skewered by his ski pole three days into their honeymoon, nearly finished her off just when she thought she was safe at last. After Cousin Harriet left, I searched my mother's nightstand and her drawers, understanding that she had a past and had a self that came before me, but I never found a picture of Stan Muslic, nor one of Margaret Brown Muslic before she married my father.

I pressed my mother for details of Life Before Sol and found out only that she left Ithaca after a few years and studied art. This is what I made up: She sketched at night while lying on her pallet in the chicken coop and lived on the table scraps of the large and vile Muslic family. She sent away for art books with her egg money. Unable to endure their harshness, their obesity, their utter lack of manners, she fled to New York City, where she fell in love with garmentos, labor union organizers, knock-off Dior suits, and anonymity. She supported herself buying and selling antiques and reproductions and fakes. For herself in those early years, she bought only sketches from up-and-coming artists and two elegant, witty Limoges boxes, one of a hot-air balloon, one of a white-and-gilt piano with a single black note painted inside. She gave me the boxes instead of a bat mitzvah.

Margaret was twenty-six, with a nineteen-inch waist and a one-bedroom apartment in Greenwich Village, when she met my father. In my version, she looks a great deal like a blonde Vivien Leigh before she lost her marbles. The men she met must all have been married, or losers, or something worse, because she became fond of my father during his twenty-five-minute lunch breaks from Phillips, Kritzer and Kahn, the best firm a young Jewish accountant could join in 1953 (as he told me a hundred times). She let him browse among the antiques as though he belonged there, and let him look at her as though his interest was not absurd. He must have thought she was the answer to his prayers, the shield for his defects: naturally thin, naturally blonde, obviously English (meaning not Jewish), and artistic (meaning sexy) without being hysterical.

I don't know what my mother thought. Her bravery had limits; she believed that marriage provided camouflage and safe passport, that she was at risk without it. I don't say she was wrong. I just wish she'd stayed single a little longer, looked a little further. Sunday mornings I sat in front of the TV, watching cartoons and reading in my pink, pilly robe. I licked the corners of my mouth until they cracked and bled, pressing them dry on a tissue. My father threw *The Saturday Evening Post* across the room, saying I was "just like Aunt Freda, for God's sake." When I tired of imagining my own dead body sprawled at the bottom of the front hall stairs, I pictured him crushed to death by Great-aunt Freda and her sister Aunt Dorothy and their brother Uncle Izzy, all relatives I'd never met, left behind in the villages of Poland and the chicken farms of New Jersey.

* * *

My mother left me alone in the bathroom for about an hour. Finally, I figured out that you had to take the cardboard off before you used the tampon, and after that, my period was boring. I didn't bleed much, and I didn't smell too bad. I actually liked the smell of iron and salt. I didn't keep a little calendar like some girls, so I ruined about twenty pairs of panties that year and took to carrying extras in my schoolbag, along with six tampons, Maybelline Frosted Peach lipstick, Lush Lash mascara, Midnight Pearl eyeshadow, and a Cornsilk compact. I looked in that little mirror constantly and covertly. I stroked my thighs and breasts, shaved my legs every other day. I examined every inch of my face and front, and stole my mother's pink European gels and aqua creams, sometimes exfoliating, hydrating, and pore-minimizing all in one Saturday night. I used a loofah on all my rough spots and slept on a stolen satin pillowcase to combat premature wrinkling. I bleached the tops of my toes so that when I appeared on the Riviera, Sean Connery would not be disgusted by the sight of my darkly hairy feet. I languished seductively in the bathroom mirror, using the steam and my towel-turban to create movie star cheekbones and attitude. I would not say it to anyone (who would I say it to, even if I'd been willing?), but I thought I had potential.

In ninth grade, no one cared about what anybody'd done in elementary school. When Frannie Grant, *the* most popular freshman girl, was browsing with her group just one aisle away from me in Woolworth's she smiled at me, her famous triangular smile, and I picked up a bouquet of mascaras, black

and mink and teal blue, one for each of her friends, and a tray
of eleven coordinated eyeshadows, the nearest expensive thing
I could grab, and walked out of the store. I put it all into her
cupped hands.

"I have more stuff than I need," I said. "Knock yourselves
out."

Boys looked at me carefully, smashed into me in the halls,
but didn't speak. Rachel Schwartz lent me lunch money and
taught me to say "Fuck you" in Hebrew, Arabic, and Swahili.
Rachel was the only person worth talking to. When we were
in fifth grade and she was the new girl from New York City,
she invited me over for three weeks in a row. We played
Lawrence of Arabia and terrorized her mother's elderly dachshund, Schatzie, who had to wear a chiffon scarf around his
neck and be the sheik. We played Sailor, and I put on one
of her brother's blue baseball shirts and walked bowlegged
around her canopied bed until the big moment, when I undid
her bra and laid my head on her soft, custardy breast, making
sure my nose and lips didn't touch her raspberry-pink nipple.
Because of her big breasts, Rachel got to be the Lady. A few
times, dressed in her father's black silk kimono, Rachel made
me tie her to the metal pipe in their semi-finished basement
and light matchbook fires in a circle around her. She swooned
neatly, slipping out of the kimono, and I untied her and
dragged her over the cork floor to the safety of the laundry
room, reviving her with tender pinches and sips of soda. Her
head lay back on my arm, and as the Sailor and the Lady we
French-kissed, and she tasted like Fresca and the smell of
doused matches was in her hair. We read to each other from
the Playboy Adviser, whose mascot was a Bunny Tinkerbell

with fascinating, garterless black hose pressing into her thighs. Our last Saturday, we pulled her mother's stockings over our faces and pretended we were robbing a big bank and the loot was her mother's costume jewelry and all the change in her father's sock drawer. Rachel didn't call me the next day and she didn't call me the next week. I waited and smiled warmly when I saw her at school and still she didn't call. She walked around the courtyard with Sabra and Julianna Cohen, a twist of arms around waists.

By the next year she'd bounced off the Cohen girls to the most popular socks-matching-sweaters circle, and in eighth grade her picture was in the junior high yearbook eleven times, six times with boys. But in ninth grade, as I was finally figuring out the rules, happily wearing skirts barely covering my underpants and hiphuggers riding just above my pubic bone, she quit horseback riding and modern dance and pep band and got fat and angry and more weird-looking than the rest of us. She wore sunglasses and bunny bedroom slippers and mirror-spotted Indian halters to school. She called to tell me the dachshund had had a heart attack, and then she said "I'm sorry," and we never got off the phone. We played records into the receivers for each other, and occasionally Rachel played her guitar over the phone. On weekends we answered the personal ads in the *The Village Voice* and made dates we would never keep with grown men whose desperation and terrifying want could only be managed by ridicule. The more elaborate the date plans, the more specific the costume requests, the harder we laughed when we got off the phone. Given weapons, we would have been snipers.

Most of my teachers liked me, and I didn't feel too bad

about being in Extended Algebra, which took three semesters to do what everyone else did in two. If they had had Super-Extended Algebra, I would have been in that. Mr. Provatella saw that although I grasped the concepts of algebra, I had not learned how to divide and could barely multiply, and while everyone else struggled through endless sheets of equations, he and I talked about infinity and the envelope of time.

Mr. Stone, my English teacher, read poetry to our class and told me I could show him my own poems after school. I sat next to him, smelling his coffee and tobacco and middle-aged-man smell, watching him roll up his sleeves over his wide arms. He tapped a ridged fingernail over each line, circling a misplaced word, running a yellowed fingertip back and forth over a nice phrase.

I wrote poems about loneliness and terrible fires in crowded tenement buildings and poets dying in the Russian snow.

Mr. Stone said, "I know you know about the loneliness, honey," and he crossed out every other line and made me put away all the poems located in places I'd never been. I brought him three boxes of blue pencils.

Mrs. Hill and I were working our way through *Pride and Prejudice* and the story of her courtship with Mr. Hill. I gave her a couple of manicures without hurting her too badly and hoped she wouldn't ask for a pedicure. One afternoon, I found her smiling in her sleep when I walked in, her feet, brown and yellow and bumpy as toads, soaking in warm water and chamomile leaves. I dried her feet and moisturized them and filed down her toenails and painted them Carnaby Crimson.

I had everything I needed.

PEACE LIKE A RIVER

▼

From behind Mr. Stone's desk I watched the entire junior high walk by, their faces passing between my pointy toes. I drank Mr. Stone's coffee and waited for someone to admire my red cowboy boots propped up on a pile of blue books. I shut the door and read everyone's grades.

In that little office, with the frosted-glass window facing me and the view of the parking lot behind me, with the dirty metal file cabinets and the film of cigarette ash and dust and the apple cores rotting in Mr. Stone's wastebasket from Monday to Friday, I felt whole. The dreams other girls tried to make real with boys or clothes or horses were nothing to me. The best dream, the true red heart of my life, was Mr. Stone; Rachel and Mrs. Hill were the ribbon, and books were the lace trim.

When he came in, I was crying.

"Liz, what's the matter?"

"My father's moving out."

My sharply proper mother had loosened the reins on me entirely, distracted by weekly legal encounters over the Chippendale, the Klimt, and the Fiestaware. My father gave me twenty dollars every time he saw me, and offered me all the things he wouldn't let me eat when I was little. It wasn't really so bad. It wasn't tragic.

"I'm sorry," Mr. Stone said.

I think he felt sorry for us all, even for my mother, who never inspired sympathy.

"Maybe things will get a little better now. Maybe you and your mother will fight less and you and your father will spend more time together."

I didn't think he really thought that.

"Maybe, maybe not." I stared at the toes of my boots.

"Maybe not," Mr. Stone said without smiling. Sometimes he would smile when I was looking away, but when we really looked at each other, I saw the pink rock of his face with grey mossy hair on top and wild, twiggy crescents of eyebrow above his small, slanty blue eyes.

I loved him for not lying to me, but I started crying again, drops falling on my notebook. I hoped he'd give me permission to skip class. I hoped my nose wasn't running and that I wasn't ruining Rachel's mother's silk shirt.

"Can you go to class? The bell's ringing."

"I guess. I don't know."

"All right, forget it. Stay here. I'll write you a pass and you can go later. Whose class are you missing?"

"Algebra. Mr. Provolone. I mean, Mr. Provatella's."

"Well, you can't get much more behind than you are, I guess. You're not going to be a mathematical genius, Miss Taube. You better cultivate your other talents." He poured some coffee out of his thermos. "I have to go teach. I can give you a ride home if you want." He walked off quickly, a kind of fast, barrelly cowboy's walk.

I sighed and rummaged in his desk for the chocolates in the back of the bottom drawer. He loved me.

Mr. Stone drove me home that afternoon, and in the cocoon of his little Volkswagen I inhaled the smoky air and held my breath, smiling and trying to memorize each passing house, to make the trip from the junior high parking lot to my driveway seem longer.

"You're growing up."

"Yeah. It happens," I said.

"Do you babysit, grown-up?"

I had, but I was still scared to stay by myself at night. "Yes. I mean, not much," I said. "But I can."

Mr. Stone frowned. "Okay, maybe you'll babysit for us sometime."

He pushed my hair behind my ear, squinting at me through the smoke, and I thought that he wouldn't ask me to babysit, that we would never sit in the Volkswagen, driving past darkened houses in the moonlight, but he did, right before school ended.

I expected to be a good babysitter, even a great babysitter. I liked cats, I admired the toddlers at my father's office Christmas party, I cleaned up after Mrs. Hill all the time. I could babysit for the Stones. Really stupid girls babysat for three kids, even three boys, all the time.

I waited in the foyer, watching for him through the colored glass panels. His car drove through the purple, the blue, and the yellow, and at the green I went out to keep him from honking the horn. The thought of my parents and Mr. Stone in the same room, standing in the foyer, sitting side by side in the leather chairs, chatting about me, was so horrible that at night I would imagine it to scare myself, the way I used to shut my eyes and see, on the deep red screen of my inner lids, blood-tipped green monster claws hanging over the edge of the clothes hamper.

Mr. Stone didn't say much on the ride over. I wore my low-riding bell-bottoms and a Mexican blouse with lemons and oranges and red hearts swirling down the front of my breasts. I sat completely upright so my stomach wouldn't come close to my belt. He said, "Pretty blouse." He talked like a father, about his sons and what they were good at; he didn't even look my way. He said that they were good kids and exceptionally bright, which even my parents said about me. He said Danny was shy, Marc was outgoing, and Benjie was nine going on thirty. I thought I would probably get along with Marc and maybe we could watch TV while the other two played chess or read *The History of Western Civilization* or did whatever brilliant children do. I told Mr. Stone I loved children, and he laughed.

I had never seen a house like the Stones'. Later on, lots of the houses I went into reminded me of theirs, but then it was as new as a foreign language. I loved the zebra-striped door and the leather-and-bronze knocker and the brambly brown lawn. Every cliché of bohemian life was new and charming to me: the black and red canvas pillows on the scuffed wood floor, the low black foam couch on fat mahogany feet, the grey, balding rugs, and the trailing, two-generation spider plants in bulbous hand-thrown pots, their hairy green strands winding down through the macrame onto the backs of people's necks and into their lumpy, half-glazed mugs. A headless mannequin with an army cap on its neck and a peace symbol on its chest stood in the front hall. My parents had taken me to Versailles when I was eleven and I was not half so impressed. The only things I didn't like were Mrs. Stone's paintings. I didn't not like them; they terrified me.

Mr. Stone practically pushed me through the front door, and when I had to go back to the car for my knapsack, he disappeared. Mrs. Stone invited me to look at her pictures and made me cross the room with her until we stood facing them. They hung on the wall like nightmares, even the frames oddly pale and uneven, covered with worm lines and tiny brown bug holes. I could hear Mr. Stone in the other room, rumbling over the sound of the little boys and the Muppets.

"Well, now you see what I do," she said, like I'd been wondering.

"Uh-huh, yes, I do." I looked around, hoping Mr. Stone or the boys would come out of the TV room.

The biggest picture was a corpse, a woman with her belly slit open to her breasts and little creatures—I didn't look too closely—miniature soldiers and animals climbing out across her body.

"What do you think?" She reached up and put her hand on my shoulder and just left it there.

"It's trying to say something" is what my mother always said when she looked at things this ugly, but I couldn't say that. I did not want to know what these pictures were trying to say, or why Mrs. Stone was trying to say it to me.

"Elizabeth may not be ready to comment on her employer's artwork, sweetheart."

I kept quiet, listening to that complicated "sweetheart."

"All right, Max," she said, and she took her hand off my shoulder.

The boys were behind Mr. Stone, hanging on like little freight cars and wearing the weirdest pajamas I had ever seen. They were like flannel nightgowns, but instead of being navy or plaid, which would have made them a little less weird, they were hot pink with tiny black houses, grey with rust-colored stars, and yellow with blue frying pans printed all over. Danny and Marc were real twins, not fraternal, and one of them was wiping his nose on the hem of his nightie. He wasn't wearing underpants.

"You're quite tall," Mrs. Stone said.

I didn't say anything. I didn't say, And you're quite old. Or, Your teeth are quite yellow and your paintings are quite nuts.

"I designed the boys' nightwear," Mrs. Stone said.

I figured. "What time do you want them to go to bed?" That's what babysitters always asked my parents.

"Oh, let's see. Eight-thirty for the twins, I don't know, they're only eight. Nine for Benj, I guess . . . if that seems reasonable." She didn't seem to have much experience with babysitters.

I asked them for the phone number where they'd be and if the boys were allowed to have snacks and everything else that my babysitters used to ask. My parents' favorite sitter wrote it all down in a little notebook, which I thought was pretty obsessive, even though I hadn't known the word at nine. Benjie probably knew the word.

Mrs. Stone clasped each boy's face in her palms and turned around to look at us all as Mr. Stone led her out, as if she were going away for years. When the door closed, all three boys sucked thoughtfully on their lower lips, just like Mr. Stone.

"So, who eats ice cream?"

I was the babysitter I'd never had. I was better than Mary Poppins because I didn't care what kind of people they became, I just wanted to be their favorite; I wanted them to despise other babysitters. I showed them how to soften the ice cream, mix it with broken-up cookie pieces, and refreeze it. We ate a quart of that. Their eyes got big and starry when I found the hot fudge and let them eat it out of the jar while we watched *Million Dollar Movie*. We played cowboys-and-Indians-in-outer-space until the twins collapsed in the hall, and then I wiped the biggest chocolate streaks off their faces and dragged them heels first up the stairs to their beds. They had bedspreads as weirdly patterned as their nightgowns.

Benjie said, "They have to go, you know. Or else." And I got them back up for that and threw them in bed again.

"Let's play something," he said.

"Okay," I said, and took out a deck of cards in case he wanted to learn Spit or Crackerjack.

He leaned back against the couch, opened his mouth wide, and rolled his eyes up until only the whites showed. Opening his mouth made him look much worse, the wet pink hole and the brown-tipped fern leaves almost grazing his bulging, blank eyes.

"Benjie. Benjamin."

"I can't hear you or see you. You are invisible."

"Okay. You can unroll your eyes if you want. I'm now invisible." I had a babysitter who would play this kind of game with me: Let's pretend you're an animal in the zoo, you get under the table and you can't get out, while I go talk on the phone. I hated her when I understood, but if he *wanted* to play like that, I didn't mind. I picked up a *Life* magazine and flipped through pictures of hundreds of girls getting their hair cut like the Beatles. Benjie unrolled his eyes, and they were very bright and liquid, like they'd been washed while they were up there. He stood up and pulled his nightgown over his head, making a flannel column with his arms, so I could get a good look at his naked body. It was like his brothers' but bigger, and I had more time to look. His thing was like a soft, taupey cigar. A cigar with a droopy little bow around it. He kept standing there, and finally I picked up the magazine again.

"Any time, Benj."

"You are invisible," he said from within the nightgown.

"Oh, yeah. Okay, I'm invisible."

He threw his nightie across the floor and took the magazine out of my hands, making me look at his naked chest.

"Do you want to play cards? I can teach you a game."

"Okay," he said. "Strip poker."

"Definitely not. How about regular poker?"

"You're invisible," he said.

He dove onto the couch and began rubbing up against the cushions in this really disgusting way.

"Oh, Max, Max, Max," he squealed.

"Come on, don't be gross."

He kept pumping away at the cushions and finally just lay

there shaking, his little butt sticking up like another cushion, round and shiny.

"I'm going to look in my father's room," he said, and I followed him because I thought I should keep an eye on him and because I loved to look at people's stuff.

"You want to put something on? It's cold in here." It *was* cold. The Stones must have kept their bedroom at fifty, and Benjie's whole body was covered with goose bumps.

"Invisible," he said, and headed for their dresser.

Which was exactly what I would have done if I was by myself. The things I liked best about babysitting, in the three jobs I'd had so far, were the eating and the snooping, both unfurling through the evening, lushly inviting, any small wave of shame easily subdued by the prospect of being, for once, satisfied. I ate smoked oysters and caviar for dinner, having discovered that people's pantries yielded up interesting hors d'oeuvres tucked away behind the flour and the Crisco and the onion soup mix. And I ate ice cream with my fingers and shook Oreo crumbs down my throat when I'd finished the box. *No one saw.*

Benjie crouched in front of the dresser, his little thing dangling between his ankles. He held up a few pairs of his mother's baggy white underpants, more like my panties than a grown woman's, I thought, and then he put them back in the drawer. I certainly wasn't going to make fun of his mother's underwear, but if that was all we were going to find, I'd go back to the magazine and he could call me when he was tired. He held up a little plastic shield.

"Athletic cup," he said, putting it in front to show me how it worked. "My dad used to wear it for rugby."

I started looking around on my own. If I waited for Benjie, we'd never get to any good stuff. I stuck my hand under the bed, and then I got down on my knees. Under the bed and back of the closet had been the best places so far. I didn't like going into basements, certainly not for the split garden hoses, rusty skates, and used tires that everyone kept.

There was nothing under the bed, but in the back of the closet there were shoe boxes half filled with curling photographs. I let Benjie rummage in the underwear drawers. The pictures were of Mrs. Stone.

She was naked, kneeling in one, on her hands and knees in the others, looking back at the camera with a stupid smile. Her long hair hung over one shoulder, and her rear end was dark with pimples and little creases and hairs. The whole thing was worse than her paintings. I put the photos back in the box and the box back behind Mr. Stone's winter boots.

"Let's go," I said. "There's nothing here anyway."

"Look at this. It's Greta."

I hated it when kids called their parents by their first names, like they were other kids.

She is skinny and tall in the photo, taller than she looks now. Maybe it's because her skirt is so short and her hair is short too, with bangs sticking out in three directions. She's wearing shoes with no socks, but it doesn't look like summer; she's wearing a boy's jacket, her hands stuck in the pockets.

"Where is that?" It's obviously not America.

"Prague. That's in Czechoslovakia. They speak Czech. My mother speaks Czech."

"Do you?"

"A little. Not really. She looks weird."

"Yeah." I looked at the picture again. I knew what she was thinking as if I were standing there myself, my hands in her pockets, our fingers wedged together in the torn lining. She is trying not to cry. Everyone wants her to be happy now, and she's trying.

"It's late, Benj. You're supposed to be in bed."

"You're invisible."

"I am not fucking invisible and it's ten-thirty. Come on, put the picture back."

He jumped on the bed, bouncing like a trampoline expert, knees bent, arms parallel to the mat, thing flapping up and down in a blur.

"Come and get me, *milacku.*"

"What's that?" I began circling the bed. I wanted to grab him, but I didn't want to smush my face against his thing or his butt.

"*Milacku,* sweetie pie. *Milacku,* sweetie pie. *Mam te rad.* I love you. *Mam te rad. Dobrounots.* Good night. *Dobrounots.* Good night, good doughnuts."

He kept singing the words and repeating them until the English and Czech ran together and I couldn't understand anything. The bed was creaking loudly, rocking on the short wooden legs.

"Benjie, get off the bed."

"Say the f-word again."

"Get off the bed. I'm sorry I used bad language."

He started screaming. "Say it. Say the f-word."

"Okay, stop it. Jesus. Get off the fucking bed. Okay? Get

off the fucking bed and give me the fucking picture. Your parents will never fucking hire me again if they come home at eleven and find you wandering around the fucking house butt-naked. Okay?"

By the third "fucking" he stopped bouncing, and then he just sat on the end of the bed, waving the photo at me like a little grey flag. I took it out of his hand and put it back in the black leather wallet he'd found it in.

"Where'd you get the wallet?"

He shrugged.

"Come *on.* You can't go looking through people's stuff and leave it all over the place." Lessons in Rudimentary Snooping.

"In the thing there." He pointed to the nightstand.

I wasn't a genius, but at nine I knew the word for "nightstand." Of course, because of my mother, I also knew "escritoire," "armoire," and more about Chippendale Chinese than most people.

I slid the picture out, looking again at her face, skinny little scared face with a big fake smile. I put the wallet back in the drawer, laying a pencil stub across it to make it look normally messy.

I was getting used to Benjie being naked. I didn't even care when he left the bathroom door open while he brushed his teeth and peed.

I pulled the covers over him.

"Sit with me," he said. "I'm scared of the dark."

"Come on," I said. I wanted to watch TV.

"I am. You have to sit with me. Max does when she's not here."

"Usually it's your father?" I liked the idea of Mr. Stone's being a great father.

"No. Her. Because she's here. You know, she sleeps in here." He pointed to the twin bed on the other side of the room.

"Your mother sleeps in here?"

"Yeah. Is that weird?"

"No. Maybe she sleeps in here because you're scared of the dark. To keep you company."

"Maybe," he said, and he yawned.

"You can fall asleep now, you're all right. Good night, Benjie."

"*Dobrounots, milacku.*"

"*Dobrounots,* you doughnut."

SCANDALIZE MY NAME

▼

"Let's have a look-see at that right hand," Mrs. Hill said, eyes on the ceiling.

"Vivian said absolutely no more pork rinds."

I was fifteen, and in our two years we had one ambulance ride, two angina attacks, and more than a few sponge baths between us. After *Pride and Prejudice*, we alternated between the tabloids and the poetry of Mr. Paul Dunbar.

"Do you see Vivian on the premises?"

"Come on, Mrs. Hill, it's not good for you." There was no other adult I could talk to like that. My mother never did anything that wasn't good for her, my father's arteries were of no interest to me, and Mr. Stone, who knew something about everything, made it clear that we could talk about me but not about him.

"Who dropped you off? I heard a car door." Mrs. Hill liked to think that her hearing was extra sharp to make up for her eyesight.

"Mr. Stone." Very proud.

"Who's that?"

"He's my English teacher this year."

"Why's he dropping you off here?"

Mrs. Hill was always faintly accusatory. I shrugged, which I knew she couldn't see but would feel, and started peeling carrots.

"Elizabeth, am I talking to myself? Are you in some kind of trouble at school?"

"No, I'm not. I imagine he dropped me off here because I was going here." I spoke very slowly and clearly, to show her how stupid she was being.

"How old a man is this Mr. Who?"

"Mr. Stone. How should I know? Old. Do you want these carrots pureed or in circles, to go with peas or something?"

"He drives you home a lot?"

I sliced the carrots into inedible oversized chunks and went into her bedroom to gather up the laundry. She would sit and wait for me to come back. Her legs hurt too much for her to follow me around pestering me.

"Has your mother met him?"

Not on a bet.

"Your legs are getting long."

I shrugged again.

"You stopped wearing your glasses. How come?"

"Contacts." I loved my contacts. I loved the sharp world and I loved my eyes, edged in black eyeliner. I had scratched my corneas twice because I couldn't bear to take the lenses out, except to sleep.

Mr. Stone dropped me off on Tuesdays and Thursdays, and after that, I tried to shut the car door softly, grabbing it with both hands to keep it from slamming, and as soon as I walked through the door Mrs. Hill would say, "Fool," as though she were speaking to someone else.

Charlotte Macklin was the school social worker, and if she had heard Mrs. Hill, she would have felt better about me. She thought no one gave a damn that I spent all my study halls in Mr. Stone's office and was frequently seen getting into his car after school. Mrs. Macklin knew, even if no one else did, that although it did not violate any school rule, it undermined morale for students and teachers to see a ninth-grade girl sitting behind the desk of the English department chairman, sipping coffee out of his thermos, showing her boot bottoms to the passing world. Mr. Stone had already heard from her, but I didn't know that then. Mrs. Macklin looked at me knowingly as I skated past, her pale blue eyes narrow with concern, her handkerchief twisting into damp white loops. She sent me three notes, inviting me to a self-esteem group, to a girls-with-divorcing-parents group, and finally to a one-on-one interview to discuss my goals and expectations for high school. I declined, and she called me out of algebra, showing that she had not read my school records all that carefully. She asked how I was feeling about my parents' divorce and I said fine. She said she'd noticed that I preferred to have my lunch in Mr. Stone's office rather than in the cafeteria and I said that was true. We eyed each other for five minutes, and she sent me back to class. I told Mr. Stone about it, and his face got really red, which meant trouble for Mrs. Macklin. Mr. Stone and the principal were old friends and Mrs. Macklin was nobody.

By the end of May my parents were legally divorced. My mother took on a secretary, a yoga teacher, and a bottle-green

MG. She was already talking about where I would go to college. She'd had enough.

My father moved further out on the Island, to a cottage in Sag Harbor, and came by for oddly formal, oddly pleasant visits. We gave up on eating out together after trolling up and down Northern Boulevard in his Oldsmobile, looking for a place to get to know each other, silently fishing broccoli out of broccoli and beef, anchovies out of Caesar salad, and raisins out of rice pudding, and discovering that this was what we had in common. He'd knock on the door and come in with bags of Chinese food or gargantuan deli sandwiches, so fat the white paper unwrapped by itself as he laid them down, crumbling slices of pastrami and corned beef falling out the sides, shining heaps of pink meat, enough for another meal. My mother had never liked cooking, but the kitchen was her domain, and it didn't occur to us to eat in there or to put our big Polish paws all over the glass dining room table. The living room was out; I didn't mind smears of Ba Tampte Kosher Mustard on the four-hundred-year-old Turkish prayer rugs, but even estranged, my father wouldn't have it. We ate in the TV room, surrounded by enough food for six people, and when my mother walked past she shook her head, smiling politely, as if my father were an extravagant, ultimately unacceptable suitor, as I guess he was.

He stopped wearing the navy blazers and light grey pants he'd always worn to make himself look like a German-barely-Jewish-almost-a-Warburg financial adviser instead of an accountant from Pustelnik by way of Brooklyn. He stopped wearing the ties my mother bought him every year, red silk prints of stirrups and foxes and unicorns. Now he wore denim

shirts and cotton pants that weren't jeans but were nothing my
mother would have approved, and soft, goosey brown loafers,
and he began every conversation telling me how great the air
was in the Hamptons. He didn't touch me much, but when
he did, I didn't flinch. When I was eight, we'd bumped into
each other naked outside my parents' bathroom, and as he
gently pulled me off him I cried out at his trembling, helpless
sac; I felt so sorry for him, appalled that that dangling, chick-
enish mess was the true future of boys. He was friendlier, away
from my mother. She was the same. No warmer (I saw mothers put their hands to their children's cheeks for no reason and
wondered how you got a mother who did that), no cuddlier
(not that I wanted cuddling now), no more interested in my
life as her daughter than she'd ever been. My poor father belonged somewhere else, not the somewhere else that was right
for me, certainly not the somewhere else of the narrow, bal-
conied brownstones and stark glass apartment buildings that
seemed right for my mother.

After he left, my mother put the moo goo gai pan and the
shrimp in garlic sauce in plastic tubs and said, "Another shiksa
in your father's life? I daresay *she* won't have to convert."

Mr. Stone still picked me up after school most days. I was
pretty sure I'd stopped growing; I pressed my knees one way
and my feet the other just to sit almost comfortably in the
VW's front seat. I rode with my hands tucked between my
legs. I put on lip gloss in his visor mirror. Comic book rem-
nants and paper cups and cigarette packs covered my sneakers. One Tuesday afternoon, at the second light, I said what
I'd been wanting to say since February vacation.

"I think it'd be nice if you met Mrs. Hill. I think she'd like to meet you. She used to teach, I think."

"Really."

"She said she did. Here, don't forget, it's the next one on the left."

Mr. Stone said, out the window, "You know, I grew up in a place a lot like this. Mostly white, though—my God, look at those." He pointed to twin blue-shuttered houses with orderly twin gardens and bitty porches, each with two chairs and a small plastic table set with four tall pink glasses and matching pitchers. "You smell that? That's the smell of the South, right there. Mint, dirt, and cornstarch."

I led him in, describing our progress so Mrs. Hill wouldn't be surprised and pissy.

"We're here, Mrs. Hill. I brought Mr. Stone, my English teacher. He thought he'd stop by and say hi."

Mr. Stone didn't look like he appreciated being shanghaied into the middle of Mrs. Hill's blue brocade living room set. Mrs. Hill looked right at him, which was like turning her back.

"Welcome, Mr. Stone. Elizabeth's famous English teacher. Honey, why don't you make us some tea?"

I just stood there until Mrs. Hill flapped her hands a couple of times like I was a loose chicken, and then I backed out, watching Mr. Stone. He smiled at Mrs. Hill and flapped a hand too. I listened on the other side of the kitchen door, which was so thin I could hear Mrs. Hill sighing and Mr. Stone sighing back.

"Could you come a little closer? My eyesight's not so good." Mrs. Hill's sweet-little-old-lady voice.

I heard him drag the ottoman over, which meant he was sitting a good six inches below her, putting them face-to-face. Ear to face, since Mrs. Hill was probably trying to get him in her sights.

"You're not even a young-*looking* man," she said, and I heard Mr. Stone laugh.

"No, ma'am." He sounded different, Southern, not his classroom voice, not his smoking-in-the-car voice.

"Come a little closer," Mrs. Hill said. "South Carolina?"

"Yes, ma'am. Kershaw. And you?"

"Mars, Alabama."

The tip of his nose had to be denting her puddingy cheek for them to be talking so quietly.

"All the way from Kershaw. My." For a minute, I didn't hear anything. "And what do you want with my girl? You like girls in particular? Children?"

Mr. Stone breathed in fast. I wanted to rush in and hit her, and as she lay on the floor we would drive off to someplace pastel and foreign in our dark-red convertible.

"No, ma'am. I'm not like that. I don't prefer girls to women. I've got a wife at home. And three boys."

"Well, then," she said, and I thought, So there, and wondered how close they were now. I could just see a sliver of his shoe tips pointed toward the recliner.

"Well, then," he echoed. "I know it doesn't seem right. I could lie to you, that's what a reasonable man would do. A reasonable man, oh Jesus. I beg your pardon, ma'am."

I heard Mrs. Hill's wheezing and Mr. Stone's deep cough and the clock on the mantel.

"I don't do anything I shouldn't," he said.

"Except what you're thinking, and you won't stop that, will you?"

"Can't, not won't. How can I? I'm not leaving town, if that's what you mean. And that's what it would take, about three thousand miles. Could we throw in an ocean?"

Very softly, Mrs. Hill said, "We could throw in two oceans for all the good it'll do you, and you know we should, because there is no glory coming from this and this is not a conversation about forgiveness. I don't care how you end, that's your concern, or your poor wife's. You put one hand on that child, who thinks you love her fine mind, one hand, even when she's more grown, and I'll see you turning in Hell, listen to you pray for death. And don't think I won't know. That child tells me everything. So maybe you can keep your hands to yourself, and I won't have to think so badly of you. Mis-tuh Stone."

"Yes, ma'am. I don't want you to think badly of me, and I don't want to think badly of myself. I have no intention of harming her. You must see that whatever it looks like, it is love. And I have to say it is, in part, for her fine mind. I give you my word. Well, I don't have much else, under the circumstances. I would cut off my hand first."

It didn't sound like it was so hard for him to give me up and just admire my mind for the rest of his life. He didn't sound so madly in love with me that it was scaring him and Mrs. Hill. He just sounded happy to be talking Southern, the two of them purring along, word endings gone to nothing, their voices loopier and wider and sweeter than when they talked to me.

I brought in the teacups, went back for the spoons, and had to go back a third time for milk; Mr. Stone poured. Mrs. Hill told a couple of funny stories about the kids in her Sunday school class, all of them now at least Mr. Stone's age, and Mr. Stone slapped his leg and laughed.

I walked him to the door, and he said my name and straightened my shirt collar. I lifted my shoulders to meet his fingers, and he dropped the little bit of shirt he'd been holding. Mrs. Hill said of course he should come by again, and he said of course he would hope to come again, without imposing on her hospitality, it would be a pleasure.

I closed the door behind him. She was already sighing and sucking her teeth, getting warmed up for something.

"That's your Mr. Stone."

"Yeah. Do you want some dinner? Turkey tetrazzini? You've got that three-bean salad from the weekend."

"All right. In a minute. Come in here, Elizabeth. Are you going to make me shout all night?"

"No, ma'am," I said, sighing at least as loudly as she had.

The ottoman was still warm, even damp, from when Mr. Stone sat on it and told her he loved me.

"He sure does like you. And you like him."

"He's okay. He's a good teacher. He's interested in poetry."

"*Who is she that looketh forth as the morning / fair as the moon / clear as the sun / and terrible as an army with banners?* Like that?" Mrs. Hill said.

I didn't answer, just walked into the kitchen while she was reciting.

"You're in the room, you're out of the room, I know what I know. Were you eavesdropping?"

"I don't care what you know and I don't care what you said. I'm starting dinner."

"Could I trouble you for a glass of water?"

I gave her the water and cooked and washed up while she ate, which took forever. I wiped up the bean salad goop and the turkey shreds and wiped down the counters.

"I'm going."

"Be good. Be careful. You are going to thank me someday."

I slammed the door.

Mr. Stone stopped waiting for me in the parking lot. When I went to his office, there were always other kids in it, kids who could hardly read, kids waiting to show him their papers or ask for advice or just sit around with him. I ate lunch behind the field house until school ended, and watched the little kids at recess, and saw which girls sat by themselves near the monkey bars or the back steps. Mrs. Hill gave me the rosebud cup and saucer to cheer me up.

My mother established accounts with our four favorite food places and never made another meal. I didn't tell her I'd learned to cook. She offered to send me anywhere for the summer—to sail in the Caribbean, to slop pigs and make jewelry in Vermont, to study architecture in Venice. I got a job at the Great Neck Public Library and boxed old magazines and stole old books. Mr. Stone didn't call me.

In the fall I was in high school. In the middle of October I walked over to the junior high to visit Mr. Stone. I brought Tony DiMusio, who went with me everywhere for two months, until we exhausted ourselves dry-humping and made the mistake of having a conversation. I wanted to bump into Danny or Benjie in town and remind them of what a great babysitter I was, but I never saw them, although I looked in the comic book store and near the parks. Rachel got skinny again and we fell out over Eddie Sachs, who was supposed to be her boyfriend but asked me over to his basement when she was in Bermuda with her parents. I said yes and he told her what we did and she told me she would never forgive me even though it was only one time. When they passed me in the halls, they put their arms around each other and their hands in each other's pockets and looked through me.

I studied a little, went on hamburger, cottage cheese, and hot water diets so my ribs would show under my leotards, and stole money from my mother. I bought pot from Eddie Sachs' brother and smoked it under the football bleachers. It made me sleepy and compliant, and I stopped when I woke up in the dusk with my head on a rock and someone's hand under my shirt. My father moved to Ohio for six months and came back. He said Cleveland was not the West and he was still working on getting out to the wide open spaces. I told him I might not go to college.

He said, "You do what you want to do. If you start school before you're twenty, I promise you I'll have enough money. Not after that." He drummed his fingers on the arm of the chair. "I got to have a life, too, Lizzie."

"I know," I said.

I made some cross-hatching at the top of my thigh, and it hurt like hell and looked terrible. I didn't do it again. I drank vodka and Hawaiian Punch with Eddie Sachs' brother in their basement. I think that's all I did the first year of high school.

Mr. Stone wrote to me in June, inviting me to make tapes of *Treasure Island* for his junior high literacy project. I threw out the letter.

"I'm going to be really busy next year," I said when he called.

"Please. I can't do it without you."

"I don't know."

"Elizabeth, don't make me beg," he said.

FARE THEE WELL

▼

I lay on my back in the dark, Max's head resting on my bare stomach.

He said he was sorry, he meant to wait until I finished high school, but he couldn't. We always did it that way, me naked, him fully dressed, after the first time, Columbus Day my junior year. Greta and the boys were at a conference for gifted children. Max made me dinner at his house when my mother thought I was with Rachel, and he kissed me on the mouth when I went to put away the salad. The refrigerator door curved out cold behind me, and Max curved in, smelling just like he did when I was in ninth grade. I saw it coming, the hairy, fishlike opening, and I closed my eyes. The feel of his mouth wasn't terrible—a soft bathing of Scotch from his tongue, his lips two slick bars of pressure.

"If you need to say no, say no," he said. He was nervous.

I didn't say anything. What would no get me?

He put his hand on my zipper and waited.

"No?" he said.

All right. "No."

"Your no is very sexy. You know that."

That helped. I leaned back to make him come closer, and then I leaned forward to leave. I made him nuts. Pathetic. My body said jump, his said how high. If I said no, the conversation would be over, I'd just be a scared girl. When I looked straight into his blue eyes, with the long lashes, I didn't see the crumpled skin around them or the way his brow sloped over them or the deep dirty holes in his cheeks.

I lay facedown on his bed, their bed, pretending I was asleep, while he lay on top of me, touching me under my clothes. I pressed my body hard to the mattress, trying to drive my spine to it and keep some space between us. He slid his hand right under me, his fingers wrestling against me, his belly pressing on my back. My eyes kept opening onto one of Greta's paintings, and I tightened my body until it felt like wood, and finally he said, "All right, go to sleep." He was so old to me, dark freckles and grey hair on his shoulders and the back of his neck, not tons of it like those gross guys at the pool, but still. Little scoops of flesh pulling down under his arms, and lines creasing his back. And he saw how I looked at him; when I cracked my eyes open, he had his shirt and his pants back on. After that, I kept my eyes closed.

"What's going to happen?" I asked a week later, thinking that he must know.

He laughed and lifted his head. "What's going to happen? I'm going to love you as long as you'll let me, and I'll teach you a little about literature and about real music, and then you'll break my heart. That's the classic denouement." He sounded cheerful. I thought he was teasing me.

"How am I going to break your heart?"

He kissed my stomach and pulled me up, deep into his lap.

"Like this, baby." He kissed my cheek lightly. "Like this." Again. "Very gently, I'm sure."

"Maybe you'll break my heart." Half the time, I felt he *had* broken my heart, turning what was simple and safe as milk into a pool of black ice, everything familiar sliding sideways and slipping under.

"Ha. You're seventeen. Never mind the rest. All seventeen-year-olds break the hearts of their elderly lovers. Even the ones who are not half so delicious as you. Honey, I am just the first stop for you."

I was almost sixteen, and this was my favorite part; I could listen to him talk about my irresistibility all night. "What's the rest?"

"You're fishing. That's not a nice girl thing to do. The rest is your wit and your beauty and your limpid green eyes. And so on. Now behave, I can't spend all day cataloging your charms." He kissed his hand and laid it on my cheek, and I put my hand over his. His hands were the part of him I liked to touch.

"Why not?" I loved showing him my worst self because there were no consequences. He couldn't help how much he loved me. In my real life I had become remarkably trustworthy. People gave me their keys when they went away for the weekend, and returned to find everything as they'd left it, their personal correspondence undisturbed. I babysat for newborns and folded clothes while they napped; I negotiated with the principal to get permission for students in good standing to go off school grounds for lunch. I had become a student in good standing. I still had too much to hide to behave badly in public.

"I have to read these exams, and Danny will be home soon, at which time you're supposed to take him downtown to the movies. Is it okay, babysitting for us again?"

"It's fine. Danny's a nice kid." I stretched out over his papers.

"Please get dressed. I can't begin reading with your sweet little breasts staring me in the face. As it were."

I put on my T-shirt, content. I wondered what it would be like when I was grown. Two years ago he had swept me and my glasses and my pimples and my bumping, changing body into the sheer gold-trimmed gown of Aphrodite and kept me there. Everything that followed, even between us, was bound to be a disappointment.

Every Monday and Wednesday lunchtime, Greta was at her hypnotherapist's, the boys were in school, and I was under Max's black and red sheets, slightly sick from the smell and feel of Greta. Even the invisible grit in the sheets was hers, put there to annoy me and make me hate Max.

He took something out from under the bed. It was electric, I could see the cord running to the wall. He turned it on and I laughed. It looked so stupid, an egg beater with nothing to mix, just buzzing in the air and jiggling his hand.

"What's that?"

"You've never seen one?"

I pretended to shut my eyes, looking down so that I could see what happened when he got closer.

"It's pretty noisy."

"It is," he said, "it's a noisy little thing. But nice. Nice for you. I'm just going to hold it on your skin, it doesn't hurt.

None of this hurts. It's just fun, just something nice for my sweet girl."

Max put the blobby white ball against my arm. It tickled. He moved it up and down my legs, and then he turned me over and ran it down my spine.

Max said my back was my erogenous zone. It was also the only place I could bear to let him touch me. When we lay next to each other, his fingers felt slick and oysterish. They didn't hurt me, and with his arm around me, sitting on his couch, I loved his hands. They were as wide as they were long, and his fingers were thick and smooth and strong. Romantic hands, but I hated how they felt on my skin, and when I saw them moving down my body, I closed my eyes.

In tenth grade, Tony DiMusio and I got drunk at a party and I let him touch me down there, and he snagged a piece of my skin with his nail, and I was bleeding, saying like a moron, "Oh, it's okay, it's just a little cut." Like a cut in the middle of your vagina wasn't a big deal. He called me for six months to go out, I must have seemed like such a good sport, but when we saw each other at school, I would narrow my eyes and he'd look away.

Max circled the little ball up and down my legs on the inside of my thighs, making electric tracks on my skin. He turned me over again onto my back and pulled the blanket around his face like a babushka, to be funny, and threw it back to the end of the bed. He rubbed my arms to get rid of the goose bumps and tucked my hands under his sweater. The hair on his chest was wet.

"You'll warm up in a minute, sweetheart. Do you want to shut your eyes and just concentrate on what you feel?"

He straightened out my legs and tried to pull them apart. I pressed them together and smiled to show I was sorry. I tried to relax.

"You don't have to do anything, baby girl. You don't have to move, or kiss me, nothing. If you don't like it, you let me know."

He put the little ball right between my legs, and I almost jumped out of the bed.

"Jesus. What *is* that?"

"Is that too much?" He put it down and waited.

"Sort of. Like a shock, but it didn't hurt. It felt weird." I opened my eyes. I could see how excited he was, sweat rolling down his temples and his neck onto me.

"All right," he said.

I lay back down, and this time he got his arm around my hips, holding me steady. He put it between my legs, without touching me; it just hovered above me, moving the air. A little breeze buzzed my pubic hair.

"Very easy now," he said, and he lowered it to my skin, tightening his hand on my hip. It started making muffled overdrive noises as Max circled it around like a tiny metal detector. Hard waves rolled through my legs, from the soles of my feet, burning through my shins, and then right into my center, knocking my head back. I heard Tony's voice, before he hurt me: Oh, yeah, ba-de-boom. Let me do you like that.

"Oh, yes," Max whispered, a hundred times. Nothing was left of me but smoking skin, liquefying bone. My hips lifted high under Max's hand until I slammed down on the bed, released. My tongue stuck to the roof of my mouth, and my legs shook so hard I knew I couldn't walk out. I curled up deep in the covers and wouldn't let him touch me.

"All right?" He put it back under the bed. I certainly didn't want to see it.

I wouldn't talk, and when he put his hand on my breast, I pushed it away. After a while he got up to change his wet shirt, and I went into the bathroom and saw my wide, blurred face sliding around like Jell-O on a plate.

"Cow face," I said to the mirror, and came out dressed, my hands fists. Max backed away. I know he wasn't afraid I'd hurt him. He was worried I'd hate him. He was worried I wouldn't do it again.

"You are a fucking pervert," I told him, and even when it took me ten minutes to undo the lock on my bike, he stayed in the house and watched me from the bedroom window. I gave him the finger, which felt like a stupid cow thing to do, but I couldn't think of anything else that meant *I hate you.*

It was him calling my house all weekend, but I didn't pick up the phone and he hung up when my mother answered. On Saturday afternoon my mother called the telephone company to complain. Even when the repairman ran all over the house like a crazed hamster with his ringing belt, my mother following him from phone to phone, I sat quietly in the rec room, opening and closing the dollhouse doors until he left. My mother bought two new phones. Max mailed a letter to me the last week of school, which was stupid. He could have been arrested.

Dearest girl,

Your absence and distress is killing me. Please forgive me. I didn't play fair. All I really wanted was to have something special with you. I'm sorry that I frightened you, angered you, whatever I did, I'm sorry. I am sorry and I never saw anything so beautiful in my life. You took my breath away. Please at least have breakfast with me before school ends.

All my love, for as long as you'll have me,

M.

I was bored by August. Mrs. Hill's house was about a hundred degrees during the day. We had so many fans on we couldn't hear each other, which was fine with me. She gave me two more cups, and every once in a while she'd point out some handsome white guy on the soaps and say, "Now, that's a nice young man," as if the next step was for me to call CBS. Rachel and I were sort of talking again, but she had a new boyfriend, a sophomore who followed her everywhere and smiled when she made fun of his devotion. After teaching retarded children how to swim and learning how to French-inhale, I had nothing to do. Finally I called Max. I put the receiver down when he answered.

He knew who it was and called me back, crying that nothing mattered but me, and I heard my mother making a cup of tea, and I could barely picture him in my mind while he talked and cried. He was a speck.

For a long time I wouldn't take a ride home, even in bad

weather. I did good deeds and played solitaire. I read Baude-
laire and I read Georgette Heyer. I spent my mother's money
on the movies and gas and began to watch boys again and
smile at them. My body was humming, a cheerful, wild tune
just behind everything else. And then I wanted to talk about
the books and the boys with Max, and I smelled coffee and
Barbasol in my dreams, and we started again.

SPEAK TO MY HEART

▼

I was not a cheerleader, I never played team sports, and I never watched them; I never showed school spirit, but I did like the basketball players. I even watched the NBA on TV once, but they were too much for me: huge, big-veined men, hard as trees, plunging across the floor on their big bandaged legs. The basketball players at my high school were all damp skin and calcium deposits, a few good-sized, broadening young men, the rest just tall, lanky boys with cornsilk hair flopping in their eyes until it got ridged and wet in the second half, or brown mushroom Afros wobbling slightly as they ran up and down the court. The white boys got dark half-circles under their arms and big blotches in the middle of their chests and backs, but the black boys ran water. And Huddie Lester soaked and shone like rain on a moonlit night. I was tutoring a ninth-grade girl more interested in not being left back than in actually learning how to read, and we took breaks every ten minutes. During the breaks, Yolanda ran wild in the halls, jimmying lockers and xeroxing her ass in the teachers' lounge; I watched Huddie shoot hoop.

I watched them practice three Fridays in a row and finally

Huddie dribbled over as they broke up into groups of four, shooting endlessly, a dozen balls swishing through nets, bouncing against the hard white backboard and the hard shining floor.

"You like basketball?"

"It's okay. At least you have to think when you play. Or at least you look like you're thinking." Inside, I was smashing my head against the wall.

"Yeah, we think. You tutor Yolanda McKee?"

It turned out Yolanda was good friends with Huddie's cousin Abigail. We could hear her singing in the hall, loud and sweet, behind the noise of the boys. He rested his hand on the bleacher and bounced the ball lightly, looking somewhere between me and the gym door.

"You go out with Allen Schreiber?"

"No. He's just a friend."

"Jon Schwartz?"

"No. Is this a quiz?"

"Yeah. One more."

"Okay. Could you stop that?" If he was going to ask me out, if he liked me *that* way, he'd stop dribbling.

He spun the ball up on one skinny brown finger and we watched it turn, orange, black, orange. He popped it down his arm.

"How about pizza after practice? We finish at five, I don't have to get to the store right away today."

I don't know how I said anything. My ears rang yes and my blood jangled and we sat there grinning and breathless until we heard the janitor hollering at Yolanda.

"Meet you at the bike rack at five."

We were very private and very proud. We met at the fur-
thest bike racks, the ones shunned by the jocks and the hip-
pies; we nodded to each other in the halls, and on the
weekends we walked down Bleecker Street, kissing at every
street corner and looking into the eyes of people who looked
at us. I expanded Yolanda's tutoring sessions, which was a
good thing anyway, and I watched Huddie's practices like
someone with a little time to kill, sitting down so my legs
wouldn't shake. In all our months together, we saw one local
movie and ate pizza by the slice at the revolting train station
pizza joint, run by an Indian family who seemed not to notice
that all successful Long Island pizza joints were run by Greeks,
and the diners by Italians, and that the only exotic food anyone wanted was eaten on Thursday nights at Bruce Ho's and
included canned litchis and large blue tropical drinks. The Patels served watery ham, green pepper, and pineapple specials
and flat Coca-Cola, and the drunks and tired women waiting
for the Flushing and Bayside trains were the only people we
ever saw. The pizza was so bad we started ordering the curry,
mentioned only in apologetic small print at the bottom of the
menu; astonished and happy, the Patels phased out the worst
of the pizzas. We liked rogan josh and chicken vindaloo and
the yogurt shakes, which separated us once more from everyone we knew. We made ourselves invisible. We never said why.

We used every private place a small, affluent town has,
every well-kept wood, every wintering swimming pool, every
empty boathouse, and even the seven-foot-wide granite
boulders that some people in Saddle Rock Estates put in to

make their quarter-acre backyards more interesting. Huddie brought us sodas and Twinkies from his father's store. One night we painted all the little black jockeys in Kennilworth white and made out until dawn, watching for the first home-owner to discover the new ornament on his Ivory Rose–spattered lawn as he picked up *The New York Times*. We lay in the shadows of the boulders and boats and in the big blue bathtubs of empty pools and talked. Big things were happening around us, the Revolution was under way, even here, and when the older kids and decent adults finished changing the country, we would step in and carry on their work. We assumed we knew what we thought about politics, and we assumed we agreed. Brushing and braiding each other's hair, unbuttoning shirts, idly running a toe along a bare leg, we talked about our families, about our school and idiot teachers, of our great luck, of his future with the Celtics and mine with *The Village Voice*.

I forgot Max. Every day with Huddie erased him further, until the only truth was that I had had a student crush on him years ago, that I used to babysit for his kids, that he had been kind enough to teach me how to drive a stick-shift, and that I guessed (and I could even smile at this part, flattered but sort of embarrassed) he seemed to find me attractive now that I was grown up. Did anything happen? Huddie asked. No, are you kidding? I said, and put my hand on the jumping muscle in his arm. Every time Max appeared in the parking lot across from the high school to lead me toward his car for our lunchtimes, I was completely surprised. And then I said that Mondays were no good, and then Wednesdays were no good, and I would only do it once in a great while, to cheer him up, and when I couldn't anymore, I just gave him a little kiss and Rachel stood on the school steps for a whole week, her arms folded, daring him to ask where I was. He didn't belong near my body now that it was Huddie's.

Love and desire slammed us into each other, giddy and harmlessly wild as bumper cars. We were separated only, and only occasionally, by my terror of pregnancy and Huddie's inability to maintain an erection while wearing a condom, a combination that made both of us sneakily skillful and ashamed. My passion for him flooded up like white water, immediately drained away by anxiety whenever we took our clothes off. Standing in the gym locker room, surrounded by normal girls with normal desires and normal condom-wearing boyfriends, I was amazed to learn that they found, or said they found, the erect penis itself exciting. To me, it was a dull, treacherous companion to be greeted with warmth and secretly plotted against. Huddie's penis was stupid, but Huddie was not. I had to seem so carried away by excitement that, apparently unawares, I would make Huddie come, maneuvering not to let him near me until he was done. And since we were both seventeen I had to do it a lot. To keep Huddie and his little friend distracted, I learned how to bow and stroke like the Perlman of penises; I could lick, nibble, or hum Huddie to orgasm from any position in no time. As soon as he was soft, I'd fondle him gently, my hand and his penis nuzzling as sweetly as two bunnies. As soon as he got hard again, I'd slide my fingers around the slick, ridged surface and hold tight, working steady as a piston, pumping his come against the backseat or onto the blanket we carried with us.

One time, as we lay naked in the green depths of

Wadsworth Park, his slim brown back formed one arc, the spray of his semen another, a dark and a white crescent against a background of thick ferns and the violet evening sky; I had to twist my two hands deep into our blanket to keep from leaping on top of him, holding that beautiful, bucking power inside me.

The last sunlight came through the leaves overhead, and Huddie looked up from between my legs and flung himself forward, sliding between my wet thighs so quickly I couldn't roll away, as I always did.

"I want you to feel me," he said, pressing down on me heavily, from chest to thigh. "Baby, please, just a little. Just the head, that's all."

It was wonderful. Better than fingers or tongues, this perfectly shaped, perfectly smooth and full plum flesh, moving into me, moving me right to the edge of my skin.

Leaning back for one wet, mindless moment, I felt his penis move forward, balanced with me on an inner fulcrum. Instantly I saw myself weeping in the girls' room like poor Celia Sheehan, and I pushed at Huddie's hips and slid him out of me, feeling the awful cool narrowness where he had been. He came on the blanket and cursed me and began to cry, fists to his eyes, like a little boy.

"I don't want to fight about this, I don't want to fight with you. You want to, don't you? I know you do. I know it. Can you take the pill or something? You know I'd take care of it if I could."

I did know. He spent a week wearing a condom, trying to get used to it. He put one on before he went to school and he wore it all night long, but at the first grip of latex, his penis softened into a scared purple curl cruelly swallowed by a big yellow dunce cap. "No condom, no sex" took care of my pregnancy fears, except for the ones about armed and fanged sperm, swimming and gnawing through my cotton underpants, but it drove Huddie crazy. He'd started having sex when he was fourteen and wasn't planning on giving it up just three years later.

Huddie dropped me off at the Planned Parenthood above the A&P, where I met with a series of enthusiastic, slightly disapproving women, happy to have the business, not at all pleased that I was it. I filled out forms and took off my clothes and handed the forms and a Dixie cup of urine to a woman who looked so much like Greta Stone I accidentally splashed her with half the contents. I held my breath during the internal exam and wondered how a woman could put cold metal into another woman without even flinching. The speculum clicked inside me, opening me up to the nurse's eyes and fingers, not unkind, just saying "This is what you want? This is how it is." The birth control counselor gave me a free first month's supply of tiny yellow pills and a row of little pink ones to be taken during my period. I couldn't remember anything she told me that wasn't about killing sperm, and I didn't listen to the part about side effects. Breast cancer and blood clots don't mean much to teenage girls. Social ostracism and pregnancy were the only real disasters for us, and I had lived through one and was planning to outsmart the other.

I came back to the car, and Huddie watched as I ceremoniously swallowed the first of the yellow pills. He clapped and I laughed and stuck two fingers in his mouth, his sharp teeth against them, the slippery, warm insides of his lips around them.

I don't know how it worked for other girls. I know the nurse told me to wait thirty days, to use "alternate modes of contraception" while the yellow pills fooled my body into thinking that it was pregnant, blooming with all that I would have sold my soul, my real emerald ring, and Huddie's car to avoid.

I tried. We tried. We compromised, we had intercourse with every other body part, we made deals with God as each other's juices ran down our chins, and we invited disaster every way we could, short of formally announcing that having acted like grown-ups, having done right, we were now enti-tled, goddammit, to have some big-time fun. On the twenti-eth day, Huddie and I cut study hall and went to his house. On his narrow bed, with the raw plywood headboard banging steadily into the faded yellow wallpaper, with me murmuring, "No, no, no" and clutching his hard wet back to me, pulling him right through me, until it amazed me to see any part of him still outside my skin, Huddie and I stopped trying to be grown up. After forty-five minutes, we melted down, panting and numb like long-distance runners.

There was no time to shower, which didn't bother us. We had never taken a shower together. Kids have nowhere to fuck and nowhere to shower. Only adults, cheating and careful, clean up afterwards. We jumped wet and proud into our jeans, and we left his room thick with our scent of damp, salty fur, two puppies playing in a marsh, a smell that dripped from

Huddie onto me and the sheet beneath us and seeped back into our skins. Liquid as hot and thick as my own blood ran down my legs for the rest of the day, and I smiled every time I sat down and felt the rough seam of my jeans cut into me. You would have had to shoot us to keep us apart.

By the weekend I knew I was pregnant. I remembered reading about girls my age who delivered and didn't know they were pregnant until they went into labor. Did their parents really believe that? That these girls felt their breasts change into tender, painful eggs, hot as a fever, felt their bellies slope into firm, enveloping tents around tiny insistent strangers, threw up at the smell of spinach or bacon or coffee, and didn't know? I knew.

I didn't want to worry Huddie and I didn't want to lose him.

I called Max.

"I'm pregnant," I said. "I think I'm pregnant."

Max said nothing. His breath was in my ear, thick and smoky; I heard him swallowing.

"Why don't we get you a test first? Just to make sure." I heard the flick of his lighter. "Don't worry, baby girl." He didn't say, It's not my baby, although I knew he knew it wasn't.

"Okay. Rachel told me she had a test at Planned Parenthood."

"Who was the boy?" Max had never liked Rachel, and after I told her just a little about what went on, not mentioning the vibrator or the way he put me in the chair naked and just stared at me, she hated him. When we saw him in town, she'd glare at him and mutter, and once she scraped his car with her keys. "Huddie's so cute," she said. *"He's* disgusting, Elizabeth. It's sick. We should kill him."

"Zvi Carnofsky. Anyway, she wasn't."

"Fine. Anyway, I didn't mean Carnofsky. If you don't want to go to Planned Parenthood, go see a friend of mine. Hilda Ringer. She's a very good doctor, a lovely woman."

I didn't say anything. I'd never made my own doctor's appointment.

"Do you want me to call for you?"

"No, I can do it. What do I say? Do I say I'm pregnant?"

"No, you ask to see Dr. Ringer and you say you want a pregnancy test and that Mr. Stone suggested you call. I'll take care of the bill."

"Will you come with me?" He wouldn't. People would wonder why he was there with me, and it would cause trouble.

"I don't think so, baby girl. I think that would be pretty conspicuous. You go and I'll pick you up afterwards. We can get a bite to eat and wait for the results."

"Never mind. I'll go with Rache. I'll go with someone. Don't worry, it'll be fine. I won't do anything conspicuous." I slammed down the phone. I was furious until I remembered it wasn't his baby.

I wasn't happy that I had to wait three more weeks for the abortion, but the counselor at Planned Parenthood told me what I wanted to hear and held my hand when she promised me no pain, "just a little cramping." She made it sound like going to the dentist, which was what I wanted. She smiled at Huddie and looked gravely at me and handed us a pile of educational booklets with cheerful stick-figure men and women making sensible and healthy decisions. I dropped them in the trash on the way to Huddie's car. I said it was no big deal and Huddie said it was, and we fought about things that were too big for us until we got to the park, where we lay beneath hundred-year-old oak trees and said, We might as well.

HEAR ME

▼

T hanks to Mrs. Hill and her daughter, I knew as much
about cholesterol levels and heart disease as any elderly cardiac
patient. I made casseroles with a skim-milk white sauce from
a recipe I found in an American Heart Association pamphlet,
and skinless chicken breast with tomatoes and mushrooms
sautéed in a half teaspoon of olive oil. Sometimes I substituted
turkey for chicken and potatoes for tomatoes. The pork rinds
were long gone, as were the palm readings. Now we were serious; Mrs. Hill was seriously ill and I seriously loved her.

Mrs. Hill was having a pretty good day. Her skin was its
normal coffee color, not overcast with greyish yellow tones,
and we had spent some up time before her nap, clowning
around while the radio played a tribute to the Supremes. Mrs.
Hill and I could do all the appropriate hand gestures for every
song, and we agreed that Diana Ross was too skinny and bossy
for her own good. We preferred Flo Ballard, who looked a little like Vivian, or even Cindy Birdsong, who was obviously
dumb as a tree but good-natured.

I was skinning the chicken breast and then I was not.

Huddie made his deliveries and found me curled up on the

floor, my cheek on the red and grey speckled linoleum, my hands pressed to my belly.

"Are you okay? Liz, sweet, I'll take you to the clinic. Elizabeth?" I could hear him and I could smell him and the pain was not so bad but I couldn't speak. A cold rising river closed in on me, running through me, carrying only me and my baby—all of a sudden my baby, wrapped in my arms. Naked, swept over sharp, half-hidden rocks, stones scraping my feet, icy grey sprays chilling our cheeks, stiffening her soft body, pulling her fine hair with rough fingers.

My baby is dying, I thought, and I pounded on the floor, terrifying Huddie. The blood had begun to seep through my jeans. I reached inside my underpants and looked at my red-streaked palms. I crawled to the bathroom, and he pulled off my jeans and my underpants and sat at my feet, crying for me.

Cry for her, I thought, and I told him to leave me alone. He looked at my smeared hands and legs, my bared teeth, the bits of blood drying in my black hair, and he sat down outside the bathroom door and waited.

I sat and sat, feeling clumps of blood and tissue sucked out of my bright veins, pulled out of my young body, into nothing, leaving nothing. I would be old when this was over, a shell scoured clean by the waves. Huddie would be young and I would be old, as tired as Mrs. Hill. Just lay me down next to my little baby, leave us be. I'm sorry, baby, I will never think of having an abortion ever again, no matter what, I'm sorry, God, don't take my baby, don't take my baby. The cramps were almost gone, just the smallest waves now.

I asked Huddie to bring me a pair of his jeans and to take a box of sanitary napkins from his father's store. I stood up to wash myself off quietly, amazed that my banging and crying hadn't woken Mrs. Hill. I didn't recognize my own face, smudged with bad Halloween makeup, my hair twisted into dry red tips, my cheeks chalk grey. I looked away, down into the toilet bowl, and fell back on my knees, my spine broken one more time. Little curl, little baby bud, floating in our blood. I couldn't go outside in only my spattered T-shirt, and I couldn't flush the toilet. I would never flush my baby away.

Huddie came back, and I finished washing myself and put on his faded jeans, smelling of Huddie and the industrial detergent Mr. Lester used on everything. We started cleaning up the mess, Huddie wet-wiping the kitchen floor, me tackling the bathroom. Then I took a jar from Mrs. Hill's kitchen collection. A little six-ounce jelly jar was all I needed. I went back into the bathroom.

"I've got to bury the baby."

Huddie looked at me, too kind, or too scared, to argue.

"Where do you want to go?"

I wanted to go to Wadsworth Park, but I couldn't leave Mrs. Hill. I wanted not to abandon anyone ever again. I wanted to be good.

"Get a shovel from the garage. We can go into the woods behind the church."

"Behind the church?"

Well, it wasn't my church. I didn't care. There were tall pines and soft ferns and no one there on a Thursday afternoon.

"Get a shovel, okay?" All I wanted was the sweet clean smell of pine and a safe place for my baby.

Well into the woods we dug a deep, fast hole, Huddie sweating through his shirt in the afternoon sun. We laid the jelly jar down, wrapped in plastic, wrapped again in tinfoil, and we covered it up and smoothed out the dirt.

"We ought to tamp it down more. So it's solid," he said, not looking at me. And we stamped on it with our sneakers and threw pine boughs and decomposing leaves over the space.

When Mrs. Hill woke up, I was sleeping on the couch, my feet in Huddie's lap. He wouldn't leave, even though he had other deliveries to make.

Mrs. Hill, who couldn't remember the day of the week or whether or not she'd eaten, looked at my face, at the sheets of newspaper I'd put under me to protect her ugly blue brocade couch, at Huddie's hand on my leg, and knew.

"That you, Horace Lester? You delivered my groceries already, haven't you?"

"Yes, ma'am," Huddie said, not moving.

I don't think my mother knew Huddie existed. Huddie's father knew there was someone, but he didn't know it was me. Huddie delivered to Mrs. Hill once a week, but I didn't think Mrs. Hill had ever caught a glimpse of us together. I was the one who was blind, thinking we were invisible. Huddie and I sat there, watching our fates juggled by a crabby old lady with bad eyesight and severe self-righteousness.

The doorbell rang, and I could hear Mr. Lester's rough voice calling for Mrs. Hill. She shuffled off to the door and he bowled in past her, his round face hard and black, his leather apron shiny and tight over his big chest.

"Horace, you *are* planning on finishing your deliveries, aren't you? I've been looking for you for the last hour. Miz Hill, do you need any more of Horace?"

"No, Gus, I don't. I do appreciate his coming by and all. It's a big help."

Huddie had taken his hand off my leg at the sound of his father's voice, and I had thought of jumping up, but we stayed on the couch, frozen, committed. I wondered if we were all going to pretend I wasn't there. Mr. Lester's eyes were red pin dots in his black, pitted face, and I wondered how anyone so butt-end ugly could have produced someone as perfectly formed as Huddie.

"You know Elizabeth Taube, the girl that helps me out on Tuesdays and Thursdays, don't you?" Mrs. Hill sounded like my mother at a bridge party, gracious and wary and ready.

"No," said Mr. Lester, clearly knowing, right then, who I was. "Sorry to have barged in, but I do need my boy back at the store. Horace?"

Huddie rose like a six-foot puppet, and I saw Mr. Lester's big hands come down on his shoulders. I winced, and Huddie made two fists and put them in his pockets.

"Say good-bye," whispered Mrs. Hill.

"What for? He didn't even say hello to me." I was not showing off my good manners for Mr. Lester.

"To Horace, say good-bye to Horace."

"Good-bye," I called out in confusion, and I saw the gold-brown tips of his fingers waving, his left thumb and forefinger forming the letter L, for Love, for Liz, as he walked beneath the kitchen window, picking up his bike. I knew he'd heard me.

Mrs. Hill fell into her recliner as I sank back on the couch, keeping my muddy sneakers propped up on more newspaper. She looked at the clock and picked up the phone. I was amazed to hear her tell my mother that I seemed a little unwell, that I was welcome to spend the night, and that she would enjoy my company. Her voice was smooth and bright and almost accentless, and I wondered how she turned it on and off.

Mrs. Hill shut her eyes.

"I said say good-bye because he'll be going away. Gus has family in Alabama. You see Horace again this year, pigs'll be flyin'."

Mrs. Hill couldn't palm-read worth a damn, and her predictions about the weather were completely cockeyed, but she was right about this. I didn't see Huddie again for seven years.

PART II

SAVE LOVE, CATCH LIGHT

▼

In Mars, Alabama, at seven-thirty a.m., Uncle Burf's pale blue shirt, warm and stiff from Aunt Arlene's iron, was already showing a long wet triangle down the back. The sleeve creases would stay sharp until lunchtime. Burf looked out from the post office window at the magnolia pyramids, three in a dark-green glossy row, each one starred with one lingering white flower right near the top. The only good things about Alabama, Burf said, were the vegetation, the fishing, and the food. Lately, Arlene packed every lunch as if he were going on a long train ride: three pieces of chicken, a peach, a slice of sweet potato pie. He'd get his own soda. Gus would eat like this too if he was still living here. Gus's boy ate to live but nothing more.

Arlene was in the kitchen like all three kids were still home, pulling out old cobbler recipes and stewed rhubarb and new things from magazines like spinach lasagna and barbecue turkey. And the boy sat there like who died, which was fair, Burf thought, but hard on Arlene, who was cooking up a storm, out of kindness, and hard on Burf, who was practically eating for two, to show appreciation to Arlene. And especially hard to watch the boy sickening right there at the table, knowing that he, Burf, could expect to find a letter, every single goddamn day another letter from the boy to his girl, and would have to tear it in quarters and throw it in the wastebasket during lunch break.

He read the first one all the way through and breathed in the love, that hot, hurting feeling under your ribs, love that made him sneak out of his barracks and slide past his cracker sergeant, risking court-martial for one of Arlene's kisses through a chain-link fence, going to sleep with a rust-flecked diamond pressed into his face. Love that made life matter, even when you were just looking back at it.

April 2, 1970

Dear Elizabeth Ann,

I love you. I LOVE YOU. I'm in Mars, Alabama. I don't know if you can get a letter to me. Maybe if they don't know it's from you. Can you mail it from the city? I don't think they'll check a letter that's not from Great Neck.

My aunt and uncle are nice folks, I haven't seen them since I was little. He's my father's brother and there IS a physical family resemblance, which means that Nature has NOT favored him.

Dad put me on the plane so fucking fast you wouldn't believe it! I guess you would, you know Gus. School here lets out in early June. We're way ahead of them and I don't have to do any work. The team's not bad and I'm forward. They're all big, bigger than me, as always, but slow. These are some slow-moving country motherfuckers. Because this here is the country, girl. Which is how

*they all (like y'all) talk. They all think I sound funny so by the time
you see me—whenever that is—I'll probably sound like Uncle
Remus.*

   *I want to call but they'll see it on the phone bill and I can't
call you collect, unless we set up a time. I don't have any money.
If you write a certain time that you'll call or I should call, like
Friday afternoon, between 2 and 4, before they get home, I could
be here. You have to know how much I love you. Write to me
Call me.*

   From your forever loving, H.

Burf kissed the letter for Huddie a minute before he tore it
up, and he tried not to read the rest of the letters all the way
through. He watched for letters from the girl, although there
couldn't possibly be any; he hoped, even as he tore Huddie's
letters into sorrowful, greasy strips, that somehow she would
get them and write back. No.

   Burf pictured Elizabeth Ann as a pale, pink-lidded blonde,
like the little white girl who worked at the post office during
holidays, until he remembered that Elizabeth was Jewish. Like
Anne Frank, then, sad velvety eyes and dark hair in neat
waves. When Burf's oldest girl brought the book home, he sat
down in the upstairs hallway, on his way to the bathroom, and
read it through, then cried in the shower and went to work.
Burf knew Gus thought the girlfriend's being Jewish made it
worse, but it didn't seem so; life's heartbreaks were just that,
Jewish or not.

   Nadine Taylor's parents certainly hadn't wanted her to
marry his coal-blue ugly brother. Ugly, mean, poor, no people

to speak of, no manners. Nadine's people were Maryland-based, all kinds of educated freedmen whose every historically significant letter, laundry list, and poem was nicely framed in oak and hung in every one of the Taylors' thirteen rooms; and Indians, not just high-yellow, high-cheekboned black folks, but real Weapomec Indians from Raleigh, back when black people thought that was an improvement. There had even been a French farmer and an Irish parlormaid, laying the bones for a summer house at Highland Beach where tall, barely tan men and silky-haired, long-nosed women lounged in pristine summer whites.

Augustus and Burford had only their half-mad wandering mother and their Aunt Lessie, whose sense of duty made her gather up the clothes their mother had scattered in the yard, and whose will got their mother settled down in the back room, supper on the table, and their behinds off to school the next morning for the first time in a week. Their father, handsome and sharp in his gold-framed photograph, was in the merchant marine and stayed there. Educated, beaten, washed, and brought up to respect the Lord and people who paid their bills, Gus and Burf were good boys. And still they broke their aunt's heart and worried her sick. They loved the water. White man's sport or not, they sailed, canoed, kayaked, and even water-skied. They snuck into the country club at night to swim in the aquamarine Olympic-size pool. They borrowed skiffs and returned them in the early morning; they crewed on big sailboats for reckless white boys with more money than sense. Gus kept three signed photographs of Esther Williams under his mattress and shook over them at night for two full years. Burf dreamed of deep-sea fishing, pulling in marlin with his feet braced against a mile of Philippine mahogany.

He fished religiously still, tying flies for his evening meditation. He showed the boy a few times, but Horace was all thumbs with the flies and bored wild, paddling his amber feet over the side like a little kid, humming radio songs.

"We don't catch, we don't eat," Burf lied. The boy could see for himself that Arlene had stuffed the freezer to the top with pies and stews and foil-wrapped batches of biscuits, just in case. "This here's dinner."

"I don't care. I'm not hungry," the boy said, his lower lip curling out. Queen Nadine's boy, all right, from his pink pouty lip to those long skinny feet and round froggy toes flipping through the still water.

Burf sighed. "I know you ain't hungry. Your Aunt Arlene knows you ain't hungry. All Mars knows you ain't hungry, boy. Whyn't you get your feet out of the water and we'll catch something and go home. We don't need to make a good time out of this."

Arlene cleaned the house, getting ready for the heat and wondering about the girl. Gus was crazy to send his boy away just three months before graduation. Maybe she looked like Nadine. Gus couldn't look on that face, even in white, with a clear conscience. Nadine Taylor had left behind a nice life for Gus. (Arlene still remembered the hand-embroidered underthings, the tennis clothes Nadine unpacked, blushing, and put in a bottom drawer.) Oh, Queen Nadine. Too good for Gus, too good to leave them all so young. And it wasn't high hat and airs, either. It was true goodness, the goodness of her soul, and it shone right out at Arlene every day and night now, at breakfast and dinner, sitting directly across her kitchen table and sickening.

The boy went to college in late August. Burf and Arlene watched his games on TV, and Burf thought that maybe the girl would see Horace play and write to him. Write to him, Burf thought, don't forget. Find her, Arlene thought.

ONLY BELIEVE

▼

Elizabeth was back for the last three months of school, sooty eyes and lank hair, but back. She wouldn't look at Max, lurching through the halls like a wounded man. She wouldn't meet his eyes, crusty and egg-shaped behind his glasses, and she drew in her breath when his hands came too close. He was functionally drunk every weekend and putting vodka in his orange juice at breakfast. He got himself to work, he kissed his children without exhaling, he gave a passing grade to any student whose parents would have come in to complain. He didn't fall down, he didn't break things, and he refused to drive with the boys for fear of killing them. Greta would not get in a car with him after four o'clock on Friday. The boys rode their bicycles into town, and Greta had begun to give Dan money for groceries. Max couldn't do other than what he was doing, so he bought Dan a wire basket for his bike and all the comic books he wanted.

"Hey there, Elizabeth, welcome back. How've you been? Have you finished that paper on Edith Wharton?" Manic with despair, he sounded nothing like himself; the voice he'd used with her and hundreds of students and their parents and his own children, the sound of compassionate authority, shriveled in his throat. Rachel stood guard three feet away.

Elizabeth shook her head at Rachel, who edged a little farther down the hall and sat at the bottom of the staircase.

"I'm okay. I lost the baby."

"I know. I'm so sorry, sweetheart. Was it awful?"

He tried to steer them toward his office, but she clung to the wall like a hostage.

"No, I lost the baby. It died. I didn't have to have it killed."

Max reached up, pulling handfuls of air.

"You miscarried?"

"That's right."

"I'm sorry."

"Yeah, so am I. I'm sure the baby's sorry too."

And Max kept talking just to talk. Trying to turn what they had into a bold, star-crossed romance, love's honorable defeat, as if the two of them had wept in each other's lap on the floor of Mrs. Hill's kitchen. Elizabeth said nothing. She saw his thoughts and closed her eyes. Max kissed her forehead, kissed her right through her unwashed bangs, and leaned back against the wall beside her.

"Where's the boy?"

She shrugged, and he thought it would be nothing to break her jaw.

"The boy. The boy who got you pregnant. Where is he?"

"He's gone. His father sent him away."

"Well, I'm still here, sweetheart. You call me if you need me. Just call me."

Elizabeth slid along the cinder-block wall, shouting, "I'm coming. Wait up," and when she was halfway down the hall and safe by Rachel's side, she called back to him, "Uh-uh. No thanks, Mr. Stone. Thanks anyway."

And he saw her speak quickly to Rachel, her arm around her friend's waist, and they glanced back at him and broke into sharp, disbelieving laughter.

Max had thought of affairs, normal men's affairs, as a kind of Tabasco for the ego and libido, a little zip for the everyday burgers and scrambled eggs. His own affairs now seemed impossibly lighthearted and kind, the motels pink-and-gold operetta sets, all unhappiness and endings hidden by heavy, friendly thighs around his waist, a good-natured soft throat swallowing wine, a slightly slack belly becoming round and tight under his fingers. This, this girl, was poisoned water in a thousand-mile desert, and he must drink and know he's dying.

That first terrible summer without her, two years ago, he drank Scotch until the back of his head pressed so tightly on the front and his mouth was such a compost heap that he had to stop for three days, and then he switched to dry white wine, buying it by the case. He felt good whenever he saw one of the pretty labels in a restaurant or at someone else's house, and he told people it was a great wine for the price. (Not that Max and Greta were invited much anymore. Max had always been the charmer, the half of the couple that people wanted to have over. A sad, charmless drunk and a religious agoraphobic are not much in demand at dinner parties and barbecues.) He felt, as drunks do, that if other people drank the stuff for legitimate reasons, he might, too.

After the formal yielding to Mrs. Hill and his conscience, vanquished in that overstuffed blue parlor, he had stayed away, hoping that such visible goodness would be rewarded, that he would become who he had been. Elizabeth had stayed away for months more, finally walking into his office with a handsome Italian boy, with carefully torn T-shirt, incomprehensible speech, and long black curls. Max thought, He's not really her boyfriend, she's just hired him for the afternoon, to torture me for staying away from her, which I had no right to do and which I swear to God I will never do again.

So beautiful, Max thought. Am I supposed to be ashamed for being such a dirty old man, another Humbert, disgusting in my obsession? I try to imagine the man who would not love her, the cold-hearted pervert who could look at her without passion. My deadpan baby doll, as beautiful as the day, and when I compliment her on the arrangement of red roses appliqued across the ass of her jeans, she blushes so deeply the sheer white of her T-shirt pinkens. I know she's only fifteen, for Christ's sake. I offend myself, never mind the world. Fifteen. I looked at her the first time and I wanted to pull her to me and make love to her with such tenderness and skill that even God would forgive me. And then I would kill myself, because I know I would never be forgiven, least of all by myself.

Instead of saying that every time he saw her his thoughts were of gentle fucking and violent death, Max shook Tony DiMusio's small hand and made pleasant, avuncular inquiries. Tony demonstrated interest in Max's stick-shift Volkswagen, and they argued equably about cheap versus expensive cars (Elizabeth and Tony thought cheap was morally superior; Max had been poor and they had not) and stick-shifts versus automatics (they shared a preference for stick-shifts, even though Elizabeth and Tony didn't drive).

They didn't talk about literature; Max assumed that Tony didn't read. He knew Tony could make out street signs and menus without assistance, but he didn't *read*. And he hated Bob Dylan (Elizabeth had made Max listen to *Bringing It All Back Home* eleven times just last year, and what he did not find sophomoric and obvious amused him, even as he was tempted to point out to Elizabeth all of her wunderkind's plagiarism), because Dylan was so fuckin' serious, man, and Tony's life ambition was to own a cherry-red Porsche with four on the floor, man, and just groove. So Max knew just what they had in common and knew why she'd brought Tony for a visit, and he played dumb through to the end, expressing admiration for Porsches, disdain for Bob Dylan, and best wishes for their future happiness. He believed, furiously, that he had acquitted himself well, even admirably, and that Elizabeth got what she came for.

Tony's hand was on the doorknob and Elizabeth had dropped her flat-lipped kiss on Max's cheek when Max surprised them all with a wild cruel lie: Greta and I are thinking about having another baby, I think we really will. Elizabeth lost her color and left, and Max had another year of no Elizabeth at all, in which to repent.

A whole year in which to slide right out of the Little League games, clarinet lessons, food fights, animal-filled movies, and endless doctor appointments that make up family life, into a sea of terror and lust so bright it seemed like the love of penitents for the Lord. Danny played two sports every season. Benjie, who would become Ben by the end of the next year, sat in the corner of whatever room Max was in and watched him. Benjie was Max's conscience, the repository of his own burnished childhood virtues and the one who got the five-dollar bill Max waved around for assistance before he lay down on the couch. Benjie took the five bucks, untied his father's shoes, and put a pillow under his head. Benjie had three accidents on his bike, breaking his arm, his collarbone, and two ribs, and each time he winked up at the doctors with Max's own look of jovial despair. Marc hid candy in his room and drew small-headed superheroes and screaming girls.

Greta didn't see how sick Max was and he didn't tell her. Her phobias and her exhausting efforts to overcome them (hours sweating in the living room, just visualizing the airport; near-death experiences on line at the supermarket) distracted her from almost everything. Max believed fatherhood was his drop cloth, that his true, dissolving self was hidden from everyone but Benjie, who saw, but could not, thank God, understand. Since Greta's official return from Benjie's room (two minutes of Pyrrhic marital triumph: Greta admitted her presence made the boy nervous; Max's mouth trembled with mean words and near satisfaction—then, what kind of father gives his boys *this* mother? and there were no words and no satisfaction at all), they took turns clinging to the bed edges. They had not encountered each other once, not for one minute, during any one night.

Elizabeth had stretch marks on the crests of both hips, and Max remembered her long torso, saw her ivory peach ass across the classroom ceiling. Delicate raspberry streaks forked through the creamy resilience of closely layered, glossy cells, the inimitable, intimidating bounce of sixteen-year-old skin. Nothing at all like the serious striated rips along Greta's belly, permanent incursions of painful change, selflessness burrowing deeply into beauty and consuming it. All that was left of poor Greta were those shimmering, heroic coils, nothing like Elizabeth's ignorant smoothness, nothing like the plain pale marks Max saw along his waist, quietly ugly creases he could barely make out above his buttocks when he stepped out of the shower. Max had a bottle of very cheap Scotch in the bathroom closet, for emergency mornings. It was Scotch because there were emergencies, and it was cheap because he liked to think that he might decline really bad Scotch, and also because, whatever he was unable to do, he was saving seriously for three college educations on a teacher's salary. When he woke up thinking of Elizabeth, feeling her breasts beneath his fingers, cool, gorgeous piles of loose peony, he took three quick swallows before he stepped into the shower. In the steam, he avoided the sight of his own body, a series of widening, slickly unhealthy rolls, his dick invisible, properly ashamed, appropriately dwarfed by beer bloat, a Scotch pregnancy, his own fat breasts sloping softly under greying chest hair that was losing the battle, like the rest of him. Elizabeth's breasts offered nothing, not comfort or food or rest, they were just beauty barely set without any purpose at all except their own sweet life. He'd gotten more sustenance from a hamburger, more genuine care from Greta, and more rest from a nap on the bathroom floor. There was a paper cup dispenser in the bathroom, for the kids. Drying off, Max had an emergency Dixie cup of Scotch before he brushed his teeth.

Falling in love for the first time at forty-six was foolish and unnerving and wrong. It was not romantic. Forty-six-year-old emotional virgin. Just that was bad enough; Max had always felt an easy, cynical affection toward his passing desires, relieved admiration for his own unassailable paternal love. He knew, without wanting to know anything, that he was holding on by less than a finger, and when it was too hard to hold on and he found himself laying his cherished Walther P-38 in his mouth, swallowing traces of oil and steel, he decided, as people often do when they have backed themselves into bravery, that he would rather die leaping than clinging and that there was some possibility of safe landing after the leap and none at all on the crumbling ledge. He called her.

"I'm going to be really busy next year," Elizabeth said.

"Please. I can't do it without you," he said.

"I don't know."

"Elizabeth, don't make me beg," Max said.

She walked into his office a full year more beautiful, so lovely he laughed and felt sorry for them both. She smiled tentatively. Max had no idea how she really looked anymore. Her dream face, the pale, sweet, wide-boned face that floated in front of him at three in the morning, slid right over her actual sixteen-year-old features, and if she had acne or ritual scars or a pair of tattoos, he wouldn't see. He did see the clothes. Green tights, denim miniskirt, stamp-size, undoubtedly snuck past Margaret—her mother would not tolerate that kind of vulgarity, nor would Max, at least not on a daughter of his—and a shapeless green turtleneck, which nevertheless clung to her nipples. His genuine efforts at kindness toward Greta, his late-night examinations of his soul, his frequent forswearing of Scotch, were revealed as transparent, feeble attempts to avoid the truth; the truth stood in his doorway, one foot resting atop the other.

Max didn't dare stand up to say hello; he waved her in, his

face so fiercely distant Elizabeth almost changed her mind.

"I can help out on Wednesdays," she said. "Can you teach me how to drive a stick-shift?"

You have to, she thought. You love me and I came back.

It was possible she mumbled something perfunctory about having been busy last year, which he ignored, saying only that he was glad they'd be working together and that he could probably teach her, said it with as much reserve as he could manage, even finished grading a paper as she waited, showing her who's boss while he wondered in what state they might be allowed to marry.

Max thought, If I love her after three hours' hard riding on my clutch, surely I have proven, even in the eyes of the Lord, that my love is pure. Fairly pure. Her skirt creased up into her emerald-green crotch as they jerked and crunched down side streets, narrowly missing not only a school bus but Benjie's scout leader doing a double take down Arrandale, trying to see what was happening in Max's car, this beautiful, straining, perspiring girl beside him, eyes rolling like a stallion's.

With Max's two fingers on the wheel, and his calm and constant instructions (self-control learned from years of six small hands "helping" around the yard), Elizabeth parked the car under the chestnut trees, near her bike, and they congratulated each other. He put one hand on her damp bangs, worn as all the girls wore them that year, trailing right into her eyes, and smoothed them back, astonished still that touching her sticky hair should transport him so. She twisted over the stick and kissed him on the lips, and he managed not to weep in gratitude, to remember that she hadn't ever liked his touch, and to ask her to move the car behind the chestnut trees.

He tried to be clever, but he made mistakes. He could see them now, large and plain as highway signs, but each bad idea was magic until he tried it and saw her soft face shrink to a tight screw, sharpening around the jaw as she listened. Amazing to see a middle-aged woman's disgust and pity on that lucky, un-lived-in pastry dab of a face. He'd thought he still had a chance until she'd fallen for that boy, whoever he was, doing something so right, being so right in his tight flesh and steel dick, fucking her in a way that Max could not, wouldn't dare try to with his moldering patchwork body, with middle-aged breath and clinking teeth. Elizabeth was so happy to be rid of him, there was no hiding that the last lunchtime hour was dimming affection and politeness and only middle-class manners had made her kiss him good-bye.

One three-second kiss to play over and over, for Max to hold, recall, taste the mint and salt and that fine, dry pressure on his lips, making him press his hand to his mouth a hundred times a day, for months, although even his palm felt too rough. Nothing came close except the skin on Benjie's back when he got out of the water, and Max would not let himself touch that and think of this. He reached for her, eyes half closed, hoping for another kiss, one that would turn him, not into the lucky boyfriend, but into part of her, freshly peeled, pink, all uptilted.

Gone for good.

Max watched Elizabeth and Rachel turn the corner. He left before the last bell rang. Briefcase into the backseat, empties into the dumpster. Drive home. Good, it's *Eine kleine Nachtmusik.* Milk, Cheerios, orange juice, cigarettes.

I SING BECAUSE I'M HAPPY,
I SING BECAUSE I'M FREE

▼

Sometimes God makes a mistake. Just carelessness. He doesn't check the calendar. If He had checked, He might have seen that Elizabeth was overbooked for loss. Elizabeth didn't believe in a real God, but she had a God character in her head, part Mr. Klein, part Santa. In grade school, when Mimi Tedeschi's little brother died, Mimi had leaned forward from two seats back to whisper that God took him to be one of His angels. Elizabeth almost stood up in the middle of spelling to scream. Who could believe such ugly, cruel nonsense? That God would steal babies from their families because He was *lonely,* snuff the life out of them because He needed company?

And even if there was a huge Winnie-the-Pooh nursery for all of God's dead baby angels, where did that leave Mrs. Hill?

Elizabeth lay in her bed every day after school, missing Huddie so badly her body gave out after a few hours. Rachel called, but Elizabeth was too tired to talk. Her mother hovered in the doorway, wishing Elizabeth unconscious until the pain passed.

"Would you like to talk about whatever it is?"

"No." Elizabeth rolled over.

"Are you quite sure?"

Elizabeth pulled the covers up. The only good thing about a broken heart at a young age is that you don't yet feel the compulsion to behave well, to consider your effect on others. Margaret brought a plate of square chocolate-dipped cookies and a cup of tea, which is what she would have liked someone to bring *her,* and Elizabeth wept for the Huddie-colored chocolate and ate all the cookies without gratitude, without appreciation, without any awareness that every day her mother left her office to come home, take her daughter's emotional pulse, and put a little plateful of appealing cookies on her nightstand. For the rest of her life, when people were in trouble and she cared at all, Elizabeth gave them a box of French cookies, plain on one side, a thick chocolate slab on the other.

The lady who phoned didn't know who exactly Elizabeth was, and the beginning of the call was a tangle of misunderstanding and misfiring expectations. Elizabeth didn't know anyone with such a silky, low-pitched, and definitely black voice, and Reverend Shales had not told the A.M.E. Zion Church clerk, who had not told Mrs. Hazlipp, that Elizabeth Taube was a white girl. In the end, Mrs. Hazlipp made it clear that Mrs. Hill's funeral was on Friday at one, at Doolittle's Funeral Home, on Little Church Road off Middle Neck, and that Dr. Vivian Hill had indicated that Elizabeth was, of course, "welcome to mourn the passing of Sister Hill." She was not so welcome that Dr. Hill had called directly, but Mrs. Hazlipp offered that it was a very difficult time for Vivian

Hill, what with losing her mother and what with her very busy medical practice in Los Angeles. Elizabeth nodded, unseen, and agreed to everything, not sure that she was allowed to say how much she had loved Mrs. Hill.

Three church Stewardesses went right to Mrs. Hill's house. They went about their business, tidying up, remarking, wrestling the smell of death out the door, humming melody and harmony for their favorite hymns. No one knew what Mrs. Hill's favorites were. When Mr. Hill died, all her sociability went with him. No Missionary Society, no Board, not even the Four Seasons Tea or the community potluck could get her back to church. The Stewardesses were not cleaning for Mrs. Hill, they were certainly not cleaning for hincty Vivian Hill, graduated first in her class from North Shore High School, went to medical school in California, *left* an ailing mother, *hardly* visited, couldn't be bothered with the church when she did. They were cleaning for the Stewardesses, for their sense of what was right, for their own peace of mind. No one would say they had not done right by Sister Hill, least of all Miss Vivian in that white Mercedes.

Elizabeth went to the funeral as properly dressed as she could stand, expecting warmth and light and a huge, swaying choir of sweet black voices, Mrs. Hill's community, her people, throwing their arms around Mrs. Hill to take her in and carry her home, laying her head on a soft dark breast.

The funeral parlor was not large. Dusty olive-green velvet drapes hung down behind two tottering plant stands crowned by massive pink and yellow gladioli. The front rows were empty except for a single woman wearing sunglasses, a chic black silk suit, and black patent leather heels. She was the only woman without a hat, with close-cropped natural hair, and when a large church lady in a grey dress and matching jacket and an ivory grey-feathered turban sat down next to her and put one gloved hand on her dark, ringless hand, Elizabeth could see that Dr. Hill was an outsider too. There were no other white people, and Elizabeth headed toward the back, away from the casket, away from the light bouncing off Reverend Shales as he began to rumble informally beneath the organ wheezing through "God Will Take Care of You."

Someone put a pamphlet in Elizabeth's hand, and she looked hard at the tiny xeroxed picture of a middle-aged Mrs. Hill frowning back, even then cocking her head a little. The lady in the grey dress got up, smoothed her white gloves, and stood foursquare in the room. She sang "Just a Closer Walk with Thee," and Elizabeth closed her eyes and tried to feel and smell Huddie in this warm, scented room of brown flesh that was all not him. The voice was sweet and full of feeling, but it was not feeling for Mrs. Hill. It was the singer's love for her Lord, her powerful, in-the-very-core-of-her-being belief in her personal relationship with her Savior, and it was her devotion to Reverend Samuel C. Shales. Mrs. Hill was only an opportunity to celebrate, and the celebration of this whole world that was not Elizabeth's and not open to her, the slap-obvious truth that this place was not her home, any more than her mother's house was, that her only home had been Mrs. Hill's footstool and Huddie's narrow bed, made Elizabeth crumple up and cry until one of the ladies beside her, kind and curious, passed her a lace hankie that Elizabeth tried to use without actually soiling it or blowing her nose on it.

Reverend Shales said all life was precious, said something

soft-voiced and tender about those who lived in the shelter of the Lord's something, and then he swung into it.

"Death reminds us that life is *given* by God, by God Almighty alone, and life is taken *away* by God. Live righteously and prepare for Judgment Day. As it has come to Sister Hill, it will come to each and every one of us. Live righteously and be *judged* righteous, for those that *are* judged righteous shall sit with the Lord in his heavenly mansions, I say they shall *sit* at the right hand of God in his glorious, heavenly home, and they, the righteous among us, shall feast at the heavenly banquet."

The women around her began to shift and nod, and Elizabeth could see Mrs. Hill nodding to herself, rooting around in the pork rind bag until she found the really crispy, curlicued ones.

Reverend Shales rose on his tiptoes, thundering now, and the chairs rocked on a tide of Amen and Yes, Lord. Elizabeth saw the straight, lean back of Dr. Hill and hoped that it was rigid with outraged love and the knowledge that Mrs. Hill was not in this place, not even held temporarily in that mauve pearlized casket.

"For those who don't live right, fornicators, adulterers, liars, thieves, gossips, the *im*pure, the *im*moral, the *a*moral, those who *refuse* to give their hearts to the Lord and those, even worse, who *gave* their hearts to the Lord and turned their backs on Him—backsliders and disbelievers—they will burn forever in a lake of fire. Because, be *not* deceived, brothers and sisters, God is *not* mocked. For whatsoever a man soweth, that shall he also reap. . . ."

The organ came in on cue and everyone stood up as the lady in grey sang again, sang the only hymn Mrs. Hill had ever sung, in her cracked, phlegmy voice. She sang it so often Elizabeth learned the words and hummed along, not wanting to intrude or do the wrong thing, until Mrs. Hill called her into her bedroom one evening and said, "Sing," and they had sat up together in Mrs. Hill's bed, their hands in a pile and night falling fast, singing " 'Why should I feel discouraged, why do the shadows come, / why should my heart be lonely and long for heaven and home, / when Jesus is my portion, my constant friend is he, / for his eye is on the sparrow and I know he's watching me, / and I know he's watching me-e-e-e,' " and Mrs. Hill touched Elizabeth's face with paper-dry fingertips and said, "You're the sparrow, girl"; and Elizabeth thought that this was family, dirty dishes and unappreciated treasures, the low friendly buzz of TV and two stiff fingers tapping her cheek, a full embrace of all-believing, all-hoping, all-enduring love in the face of deceit and pretense and the unchangeable past and the inevitable end.

Back at the house, the church ladies bustled and clucked and spread cloths over flat surfaces and laid out a ruby-red ham, banquet platters of fried chicken, roasting pans of macaroni and cheese, three-bean salad, warm greens with sliding grey-pink chunks of fatback, two coconut cakes, a chess pie, and one towering, lightly sweating lemon meringue pie. They arranged and rearranged in a serious way, serious about the food and serious about grief (of which there was not much and even Elizabeth could tell that Dr. Hill, refusing to sit down, calmly sipping a cup of tea, was not the kind of mourner the Stewardesses warmed up to), and serious about their role.

Gus Lester uncovered the chicken and sliced the ham in a

proprietary way, and when Elizabeth came through to the table, they locked eyes.

Elizabeth said, "Hello, Mr. Lester." When he didn't respond, she said, "I was wondering if I could have Huddie's address," and saw in his face the open wish to do her harm.

Dr. Hill came out of the bedroom holding a neat paper-bag package.

"Here, Elizabeth, this is for you." She shoved the package into Elizabeth's hands, and Elizabeth turned it over a few times, wanting to shake it for a clue about the contents, certain that funeral protocol could not be the same as birthday protocol.

"You can open it now if you want. It's those spoons of hers."

How many? Elizabeth wondered, and took out the nine spoons and thought that if Dr. Hill did not cry at her mother's funeral, Elizabeth certainly had no business weeping over spoons she'd tried to steal and the hundreds of cups of tea they'd had and the way in which even Huddie, banished foreer, was closer to Elizabeth now than Mrs. Hill would ever be.

"Thank you very much."

"You're welcome. You were very good to my mother and I know that having you around—"

The Stewardesses swarmed around Dr. Hill with plates of food she would have to eat and names of people she would have to thank warmly. They carried her across the room to Reverend Shales and put her in the chair next to him, staying close enough to make an exit impossible. Vivian Hill waved to Elizabeth.

Elizabeth took one last walk through Mrs. Hill's bedroom. The hatboxes were gone.

*   *   *

Elizabeth's father—who did not understand children, who had not understood his wife except to see clearly that he was not the man she should have married, who could not understand how his kindnesses were so often misinterpreted, who would not understand anything at all about love until his third wife's dyed red hair, big Jewish behind, and wide white hands knocked him into the best part of himself—understood loss. He had grown up comfortably in Brownsville; they had no boarders, they had a small parlor and two bedrooms, and he was allowed to finish high school, during the daytime. He had had a much easier life than his closest friend, Myron Flaverman, whose father cut cloth.

His own father, as reliable as a clock, stopped to pick up the *Forward* one day at Saratoga and Sutter, as he always did, and a blue Franklin from New Jersey jumped the curb and drove right through the newsstand.

Sol wore his father's clothes, sold fruit for Meyer Shimmelweiss, and slept on the couch for four years to make room for two Slovenian cousins, but he went to college. By subway, at night, dripping sweat into cheap, tight shoes, awash in his late father's wool trousers. But he did go, graduating from City College three days after his mother's death, one day before her tiny funeral.

Tucson, June 16, 1970

My dear Elizabeth,

Your mother told me about your friend Mrs. Hill's death. I wish I knew the right words, not to make you feel better, but to let you know that this—DEATH—is part of life. I recall that you felt very close to her. I remember you were always over there, when your mother and I were divorcing.

I hope she was a good friend to you, and a comfort. I'm sure you took good care of her. You will remember her and keep her alive within you, and I believe that she is also remembering you, something about which your mother and I disagree. As you know, she does not believe in an afterlife.

Your mother told me that you're not planning to attend your high school graduation. I'll come if you change your mind.

If you wish to visit me, I will send you a ticket. Please use this for flowers for Mrs. Hill or a donation to her favorite charity.

With love,
Your father

Elizabeth put the check in her jewelry box until she could figure out what to do with it.

May God forgive me.

Max said this every morning, drinking a beer in the bathroom. Clearly, his life would get much better or much worse very soon. He'd been planning a strategy for weeks. He sent her a bouquet of pink and yellow calla lilies with a note of condolence. He sent a funny postcard of a woman scolding a cat, saying "And you call yourself a dog," and signed it Max Stone. He called when he thought her mother might be gone and said, "I'd like a chance to say good-bye before you go off."

She said she'd meet him for coffee. He wouldn't talk about getting back together right away. He wouldn't say "share." It sounded too much like what he really wanted, a life forever together. Maybe he'd mention that if she was planning to be around for the summer he was thinking of renting a small place for himself, since Greta and the boys would be away. Maybe she'd like to stay there with him. Maybe he could get two places, across the hall from each other. Maybe he'd just beg her to spend the summer with him, give him two months before she went off to college and found her next romance, her next bareback-riding hero, her future husband. There was something to be said for frank and honest groveling.

Sitting with Elizabeth in a diner twenty miles from Great Neck, his hands circling her wrists, Max could not remember what he had planned to say. Her face was a little thinner. New contact lenses made her eyes brightly pink and round as little lightbulbs. She looked bored.

"I'd love to have you visit me this summer. I might take a little place in the city. Do you think that might be fun? Or maybe a cabin in the Berkshires?"

"I don't know." She made a nest of torn sugar packets around her coffee cup.

"Think it over. It's the end of June now. If you could decide this week, I could start looking. We could start looking, if you felt like it."

Max and Elizabeth shared, for twenty seconds, exactly the same mental picture: Max and Elizabeth trudging from walk-up to walk-up, meeting a dozen rental agents whose pleasant surprise at this nice father-daughter pair curdles before the plumbing's been tested.

"No, I don't know. Maybe. I'll tell you next week."

"I'll take maybe, *milacku*. Maybe yes? Is that yes for a visit or yes for—for a long visit?"

Elizabeth was done. Between his fat shrimp fingers around her wrist and the last sugar packet. Done. Now everything out of her mouth would be a lie, and she smiled like he was her favorite person.

"Maybe yes. Maybe very likely yes, a long visit. I could stay for a month or six weeks if you want, but I don't even want to talk about it for another week, okay? There's been too much going on."

"Okay, baby girl." He kissed each of the ten fingers he'd been squeezing. "Of course that's okay."

"Don't call me for a week," she said.

"Whatever you say. You're the boss."

They kissed, and Elizabeth thought, This is it, this is the last time I'm doing this.

Max thought, Yes, Lord, help me turn this around, even now, and I will be your devoted servant. Help me. The boys aren't babies, they can see this is killing us, it can't be good for them, seeing us suffer. Greta will be better off without me, she'll be more independent, she'll be a better mother, God, she'll probably recover, she'll become a counselor for other agoraphobic ladies, write a book about it, she'll make a lot of money. She'll remarry some nice Jewish guy, not to be another father, but a nice guy, bald, a podiatrist. And Lizzie and I will be like other happy couples, whoever they are, except she is so beautifully young, and we will be beyond happy, sweet Jesus, and want only each other.

Everything that drove Elizabeth crazy about Rachel turned out to be exactly what was called for in their Great Getaway. Rachel persuaded her father to lend them the station wagon, drove all the way uptown to Columbia University to collect sleeping bags from her brother and his roommate, showed her interested parents and an utterly bored Margaret the AAA trip map, and pointed out all the educational side trips and that no day's drive was more than a reasonable 250 miles. Rachel, who would become a fine doctor, would also have made an excellent president or a criminal genius. Elizabeth's only job was to be pleasant to her mother for the remaining eight days and remember her camera and a heavy sweater for the cold nights in the Rockies. Rachel packed two of most items, assuming that Elizabeth would forget almost everything, which she did, knowing that Rachel would pack two. For nine weeks they drove across America, eating apple-butter-and-whole-wheat sandwiches, kissing boys who were handsome only by the firelight of various campgrounds, and becoming expert at putting on eyeliner using their Sierra Club cups as mirrors.

Huddie lies on the gritty floor. He smells the drops of sweat spattered on the shining wood, sees the frayed plastic tip of the ref's shoelace; his face is near enough to the man's left sneaker to lay his tongue on it. Water roars through both ears. He hears only a dense, cupping sound. Huddie concentrates on these things to keep from screaming. He has to cry. The ring of fire in his right knee flames dark red up his whole side, and his flesh must be falling off in seared chunks now. Kind faces he recognizes but can't place hover over him, and he sinks into a grey minty ocean and sees Elizabeth arched back above him, white legs tight around him, their black hairs joined, green trees over them, his fists wrapped in her long hair, his face deep soft between her breasts. His mother's hand, wide, gardenia-scented, slides up his face, into nothing.

Max's letters found Elizabeth at college and she read them, the only thick, nicely written letters of her life, of course she read them and cried and returned them all, except the last one.

March 6, 1974

Dearest girl,

I won't begin with another lament. If you were moved by my misery, I would have heard from you in the last three years. I'm no longer astonished, you'll be indifferent to hear, that you ran off like that. I am not even astonished that a relationship that I thought made us both happy was obviously a burden to you, one to be shed at the earliest possible moment.

I said to you, in one of our very sweet times together, you were sitting on my lap, that you would break my heart. As I recall, you weren't in the least upset or guilty, just annoyed with me for bringing it up. And rightly so. Since we both knew what the ending would be, why harp on it?

I regret wasting even one second of those times on anger and shame and self-pity. I am trying my damnedest now to live in the past whenever possible and expect to continue doing so.

You, of course, have moved on and so I won't be writing again. I never think of you with anything but love.

Your Max

THE NIGHT IS DARK

▼

"Every couple has a life," Greta said. "Bury me."

Max stood up, staring at the ocean bleached and mirrored in the late afternoon sun.

"I know you thought ours would be a happy life, and so you are disappointed. Please bury me, I've got everything but my arm."

He put one foot out, pushed a little hill of sand toward her brown arm, and walked closer to the water.

Greta raised her voice. "Come, just a little more, Max. Just my arm. I am not asking for the world, you know, just a little sand."

He didn't move.

"I did think it would be a happy life. That is what people think. That's why they marry and have children. In anticipation of further joy, of multiplying happinesses."

"Maybe that's why Americans marry. People like me marry and have children because we are apparently not dead, because we are grateful, because we wish to become like the others. To experience normal despair and disappointment.

Garden-variety unhappiness. So, I am not sorry. We have had a normal life together."

Max was not surprised, not even inclined to argue, when Greta described insomnia and agoraphobia, sex both dismal and frightening, and the death of their oldest child as a normal life, but he was not comforted.

"Do you know what I remember most when I came here? Betty Boop. They showed her all the time, late at night, early in the morning, some channel in New Jersey. They love Betty Boop. And Bimbo and Koko. And Shirley Temple, day and night. Polly wolly doodle. *The Littlest Rebel.* Did you see that?"

"No. I was selling shoes or still killing Germans. Whatever I was doing, I wasn't watching cartoons or musicals commemorating the good old days of slavery." He came back from the water and put two scoops of damp sand on Greta's arm.

"Do the rest, Max, just cover me up."

He did, and when she wiggled two long fingers, he covered those, and when they broke free again, to show that it wasn't enough, he mounded the sand six inches high on top of her hand and crowned it with a sprig of stiff black seaweed.

Greta smiled. "You're a good man."

"I don't think so."

"I know you don't. That's part of your charm, *milacku.*"

Max smiled too; only his crazy wife could find him charming.

"I know you blame me for the accident," she said.

"I don't. We don't have to talk about it."

"You do. We do. Dr. Shein said it would help."

"It doesn't help me."

"It helps me."

"Then by all means, if it helps you," Max said.

"When I went to see Dr. Berg—you remember him?"

"The first one. Two before Shein."

"Very good. I told him everything I could remember about the camp. They were all happy memories. Can you imagine? Making daisy wreaths with another little girl, Marya. Where did we find daisies? Her name was Marya. The sun was always shining and it seemed to me that the evenings were quite cozy. We would walk to a grassy field, a group of us and my mother, and we would all hold hands and sing. I remember one of the girls had a harmonica. How could that be? We had no shoes, I know we had no shoes until winter, how could there have been a harmonica? They had taken everything. How could there have been singing in a grass field?"

Max put little shells on the sand over Greta's body, drew half-circles to indicate her breasts, and fanned out a cluster of brownish, dry kelp for her pubic hair.

"Berg said he understood, that it was a beautiful dream. You see, that I needed it to be—"

"I get it. Really."

"I was very careful in the car. I told Benjie to wear his seat belt. I told him two times. The first time when he—"

"It's not your fault, Greta."

"Of course it is my fault. I am trying to tell you what I feel about it. And you believe it is my fault. As it is."

And Greta tried to talk about the wet leaves and the square, odd headlights of Vin Malarino's father's van and the audible hesitation of sound as the car moved into and under the old maple trees. Greta heard her own voice saying *O boyze,* and then the harsh cymbaline crash of the van's left side against the front of her car, its hood flying up like one of the boys' little plastic cars and the glass showering them as the wide green hands of the maple leaves pushed through, right to their faces, Benjie's white under the red streaming lines across his forehead, spitting out bits of shiny, bloody glass until he fainted and Greta thought, If he is dead, let me die now. And he was not dead, only briefly unconscious, and as he lay on the stretcher, his face wiped with great tenderness by the paramedic, he smiled at his mother. "It's okay, Mom. I'm okay." And for one minute, she was grateful as she had never been. Surviving the camps, in the golden arms of a big American, terrible white and red acne around his beautiful smile, she was not so grateful or sure as she was in that minute with Benjie that life was hers, that she was meant to live.

"She's killing you," Greta said.

Max pressed his feet into the sand, noting the imprint of his whole right foot and his abbreviated left.

"The girl. I'm not criticizing. I'm not criticizing you or even her, but it's very cruel of her to leave you like that."

He didn't ask who, and he hoped Greta wouldn't say her name.

"What do you think? I don't see? I see. I saw. She never answered your letters, she never calls anymore."

Max put his hands out behind him and leaned forward, listening to the crisp gunshot crack of his vertebrae.

"I know it broke your heart, her going away. You haven't recovered. The mother's getting remarried soon, I heard. What is it you always say, the triumph of hope over experience?"

"That's what I say. More sand?"

"No, I'm fine. Very happy. Perhaps she's back in town for the wedding. Do you call her?"

Max kept watching the water, hoping for a few boats, but the ocean was on Greta's side. There was nothing to look at but the relentless bouncing light.

"Max, Maxie. You can tell me. Who else can you tell? You think I'm going to hurt you now? No, dearie, not now that you're in such pain."

Max felt like every B-movie prisoner of war offered a cigarette by the suddenly kindly Kommandant. If he talked, he'd get the cigarette and lose his self-respect. Probably, in the end, they'd kill him anyway. If he didn't talk, he wouldn't get the cigarette, he'd keep his self-respect, and they'd hang him as an example to the others.

"I'm not in pain."

Greta laughed, not a common thing, and Max smiled back. When she laughed, she sounded like Edith Piaf, Max's darling for the last thirty years. He has daydreams of playing Piaf for Elizabeth, and in them she sips red wine and sits without jiggling her feet.

"All right. But you're not hap-pee." Greta sang the last word.

"You said it's a mistake to want happiness."

"It is. But you do, you can't help it. And I feel bad for you, dearie. That's all."

Greta had learned most of her English from a Dover war bride in Jersey City and had been calling people "dearie" and "ducks" and "love" with Czech softness ever since. It was a thing that Max, even as he prayed for her immediate, painless death, even as he envisioned Elizabeth on Greta's side of the bed, found completely endearing.

"I think you should build a little shrine," Greta said.

"I think you're nuts."

"So? You have not been spared on account of sanity, have you? A little shrine. Her picture from the yearbook, the one you keep in your sock drawer. Maybe a few votive candles. I have those old pressed glass holders, in the shape of hands. That would be nice, you could have those. And maybe some of the letters that came back to you, the ones in the garage. That would be good."

Max sat down beside her, poking a hole for her navel and laying shell bits out in a star pattern.

"And then what?"

Greta lifted a hand carefully, balancing the packed sand on her forearm.

"And then, in your own little apartment, you listen to Mahler and drink Scotch, you mourn. You could pray."

That Greta believed not only in a Greater Force but in an attentive, specific God was another source of astonishment to Max. "How can you, of all people?"

"It's the least I can do," she said, and moved from synagogue to synagogue, praying in the back until the night they ask her to join a committee.

"Am I going to be in my own little apartment? Is that what this is? You're telling me to move out?"

Greta clicked her tongue, as she did when the boys were being particularly difficult.

"You can stay. You can go. We could keep each other company. You, me, grief. But why, Maxie? The boys are almost grown. Danny could live with you, even. I'm not abandoning you, I just think it would be better." Greta turned her face toward the empty lifeguard chair. "I do get tired of watching you."

"You get tired of watching *me*? After all these years, watching you cry at every goddamned intersection, watching you scare the shit out of the boys, watching you break a sweat just thinking about grocery shopping?" Max stopped, he didn't even know why he wanted to go on. She was setting him free. He hated living with her; just two days ago, he'd written in his journal that he was serving a life sentence, with time added for good behavior.

Greta shrugged, and chunks of sand slid down.

"I'm getting up," she said.

Max gave her a hand and dusted her off, wiping down the backs of her calves and thighs, trying to keep the sand from going into her suit bottom.

"I'm giving you the candle holders," Greta said.

I SURRENDER ALL

▼

Not long after Max's last letter, Elizabeth came home for one final weekend before the end of spring, shortly before she would have to find herself a real home. Standing on line at the Bagel Hut, squashed between two suede jackets, she stood patiently, even penitently, the edges of a pink sequinned turban brushing her eyelids. At each jingle of the door chime, everyone turned to scrutinize the next wave of customers: a pushy newcomer, sneaking in at the head of the line to make off with the really fresh bagels and the last of the whitefish chubs, or someone fondly, vaguely remembered from the old neighborhood, before everybody had become middle-aged and found themselves with expensive, youthful clothing and spoiled children. In Great Neck a woman's face or hair color meant nothing; only the backs of the hands and the little hump at the base of the neck told you the truth.

Elizabeth turned at the jingle, with everyone else, and saw Max. She pushed through the crowd surging into the small space she'd left and held on to his sleeve, making herself talk.

"Hi. I can't believe you're in here. Margaret's getting married tonight. That's why I'm back."

"That's why you're back?"

Something had changed his face. Whatever it was had torn up his cheeks, leaving them so soft and pulpy that if she'd had the nerve to touch him, skin would have stuck to her finger.

"Max, are you all right?"

He backed out of the store, brushing against the thick coats, his hands feeling for the doorpull behind him.

Elizabeth followed him onto the street, forgetting the whitefish salad and bagels and three kinds of cream cheese she'd offered to pick up for the get-acquainted lunch with her mother's groom and his sister. She stood a few steps behind Max, thinking, He is not walking away from me, he loves me.

"Go home, Elizabeth."

"I *am* going home, this was my last stop. What is wrong with you?"

Max kept going, bent over like some dark-jacketed horseshoe crab scuttling for retreat, for the absence of contact.

"I'm sorry I didn't write. I just . . . I don't know, I couldn't. I'm really sorry. Max, I'm really sorry." She yelled into the cold, garlicky air, startling two women halfway into Bagel Hut, friends of Margaret's who waved and watched as Max walked faster. Max and Elizabeth stood half a block apart, on either side of the bank parking lot where he'd taught her to drive a stick-shift, and he shouted something the wind took away, and then he stopped.

It was tears. Tears had changed his face, as they were changing it right now, breaking down his flesh with little hammers until there was nothing left but watery mass and two red wells of misery.

"No one told you?"

"Max, I don't talk to anyone anymore. Rachel's in Kenya. Is it the boys?"

"Benjamin."

They sat on the bench across from the parking lot and Max told Elizabeth about Benjamin, about Greta reluctantly, bravely taking him to his Cub Scout meeting, about the wet leaves and the teenage boy driving the van too fast around a narrow corner, one that had already been marked with a DAN-GEROUS CURVE sign. And the car partially crushed into the trees, leaving Greta enough room not only to move around but to open her door and walk out to greet the ambulance. And it looked like Benjie would recover, not even be scarred by all the glass, and then he got an infection.

"You know he had Addison's? It only seems that no one in my family has an immune system; Benjie really didn't. The scratches from the accident killed him. I moved back in; I had to, since Greta was hardly leaving the house after that. She's seeing a shrink now, the guy I used to see. The boys are in therapy, too. I don't know, I think it helps Danny, but he's the strong one anyway. Marc is just . . ." Max turned away. "The world is a terrible place, sweetheart."

She touched the edge of his jacket for comfort, fingering the little cracks in the old leather.

"I'm here. If you need me, I'm here."

"No, you're not. You're at college, leading a college girl life, and I am here, leading my life. Enough." He stood up. Elizabeth sat like a lump, arms around her legs. She shook her head, wanting to tell him it looked like she would actually graduate in June, that she'd passed all her courses and turned in all her papers, despite occasional, profound lapses in concentration, two weeklong bouts of self-prescribed bed rest, and several trials of psychotropic medications that left her dry-mouthed and dizzy, something pale green and sticky leaking from her right breast.

She had watched Rachel take college the way she'd taken the road cross-country, carefully aggressive, hardly checking the map, since all the signs seemed so clear to her and fairly helpful. Elizabeth's college life had been like her driving, too: she did it because she believed she had to (only one application, scribbled in midwinter, while standing in the post office), she never once intuited the right direction, and she understood that her safe arrival, at the end of these four years, owed more to other people's skill and sensible swerving than to her own efforts.

"I am here for you, just like you were for me. I can help," Elizabeth said, and cried into the sleeve of her sweater, relieved that she did not, in fact, know what to do, that that had not changed between them.

"Don't cry," he said, as kindly as he could. He would have been dimly pleased to hear she was graduating, dimly concerned about the blackouts, but she was alive and Ben was not and her breasts were nothing to him now, unless they could be traded, every moment of them, for him. He hugged her to be rid of her, looking forward to walking back alone, to weeping inside for Ben, to preparing for another evening of emotional heavy lifting and grey, pointless goodness, for Danny's driving lesson, for Marc's marathon TV-watching, for the balanced meal he cooked (not that Greta ate), for creating a father for his remaining, less loved boys, now desperately seeking their own lives, if only he will let them go.

And Elizabeth pressed in close, smelling his cigarette smoke and his Scotch and his Barbasol shaving cream, smells so woven into her sense of life that the sight of those striped cans on a supermarket shelf will make her eyes swell with tears for years to come, even after she forgets this conversation.

"Anything you want, Max," she said, to reach into him without his really hearing, so he'd let her in without knowing he'd done so.

"I'm fine," he said. "Go home, *milacku*."

Margaret laid out daughter-of-the-bride clothes, layering them from the peach silk skirt to the white lace blouse, an ivory nylon slip and pale peach pantyhose on top of the pile. Peach peau de soie shoes faced the bed. Idiot-proof dressing. Elizabeth drank champagne while she showered, drank stingers while she dried her hair, put on socially appropriate makeup, although not the peach-toned stuff her mother had piled suggestively in front of the bathroom mirror. She simulated eye contact by looking at people's foreheads and she fought back nausea when her mother promised to spend her life with Aaron Price, the psychiatrist she'd had in mind for Elizabeth in the bad old days. Elizabeth spent the rest of the afternoon and some part of the night in the ferocious blank haze that gives alcohol its good name.

Still drunk at dawn, she left her mother the nicest note she could and drove back to college. Instead of showing up for the graduation ceremony, she put on the peach skirt and the white lace blouse and got a job in a safe place.

WHAT ELSE CAN I DO?

▼

Elizabeth had been sitting on her knees in the cookbook section, reading recipes for things like syllabub and poor man's tarts. She had been the assistant manager at Spivey's Bookstore for the last three years, mostly because she would not become the manager. She didn't become the manager, she didn't become a teacher or a lawyer. No one ever suggested interior decorating or medicine or government, and Elizabeth did wonder, after each encouraging remark, what it was that made people think she should teach or litigate. It was probably not her interpersonal skills or her fine analytic mind. It was probably some sort of prematurely shriveled self-righteous obstinacy that people associated with their third-grade teacher or with a particularly vicious district attorney.

Elizabeth knew that the bad things that had happened to her were no worse than other people's bad things; they were pretty small potatoes, in fact, compared to terminal cancer, death by famine, incest, quadriplegic paralysis. Nevertheless, whatever effort life required, whatever responsibility for joy was necessary to make it appear, Elizabeth didn't have it. She was not drippingly miserable, she was not an affront to society. She paid her bills. She didn't smell or piss on other people's lawns. She suffered from the opposite of "phantom limb" syndrome; something essential appeared to be present, but it was not.

She thought about Max, but she didn't write. She thought about Huddie when sweat trickled down her neck, when she heard the slap of sneakers on blacktop, when she woke up and when she couldn't sleep. She stopped speaking to her mother, but not so her mother noticed. She didn't look for ways to improve herself. She didn't arrange to have her mail forwarded when she moved. She had been in her latest apartment for six months and hadn't cleaned it. She couldn't, really; she didn't own a broom or a mop or even a bottle of Windex anymore, and she knew what Margaret would say about that. It's a bad sign.

Every Friday, Elizabeth put out two cartons of juice and a bag of half-price bagels for the two crazy men who came through Spivey's back alley every afternoon, and Peter, her boss, who loved her, watched and thought, Feed me. They will always be hungry.

Cupid and Psyche were Elizabeth's favorite people. Socially mismatched, badly dressed, unprepared for the climate and the place in the way that marks the truly poor and the truly crazy, the two men spent most of their days by the concrete city fountain, a grey grim wedding cake of previous municipal good times, now barely trickling even in July and August, not even damp in spring and fall. The younger man, blond and slim, looked normal at a distance. Elizabeth had once come closer, pretending to catch a bus, and saw that he had a twenty-foot normal zone. Closer than that, you saw the heels run down to nothing on laceless wingtips, the pink plastic belt on the designer jeans, and the missing splotch of material on the right shoulder of his light blue button-down shirt. You saw his face, the features misaligned because no linked thoughts or feelings molded them. The older man was an obvious social problem, barely welcome at Dunkin' Donuts and only briefly, and only when the afternoon-shift manager felt good. He bought a dozen doughnuts at a time, never squeezing or sniffing for freshness, just struggling with the coins and crumpled bills stuffed in the back pocket of his organically spattered black pants, as wide and swaying as a Victorian skirt, barely hanging on beneath the huge doughy belly and no visible underwear. His skin was so white and his hair so black and wiry that everyone could study each individual curl around his navel. No one looked too long; eye contact could lead to conversation, and although he smiled gamely, hoping to make friends, he had too few teeth and too many things snapping and shifting in his head to have the kind of conversation people wanted to have as they shuffled through the doughnut shop, getting on with their day. But he loved the young man.

They sat on the lowest tier of the fountain, and when the sun began to drop, the fat man made a pillow of some clothes from his bag and the young man stretched out. In the damp heat, he fanned the young man for hours at a time, using a folded newspaper. Occasionally he changed hands, and sometimes he'd break rhythm to swat a fly or chase some early-evening mosquitoes. He fanned him graciously and steadily, with no unsettling changes of pace or sighs of fatigue, fanned him until it was dark, until Elizabeth saw fireflies and the black outline of the fat man's back. Then he woke his friend, very slowly and gently, a delicate, indulgent touch, and they went back through the alley.

Peter stepped over her knees ostentatiously. "Phone."

Peter had waited almost a year before asking Elizabeth out the first time. He asked again, after another year, in such a careful, casually delicate way that Elizabeth only said "No, thank you," fearing that any further remarks would show that she understood exactly what it had cost him to ask. For the past few months they'd eaten lunch together, standing up in the stockroom, putting their coffees near books they preferred not to sell, and avoiding all personal remarks (Peter lost most of his hair, suddenly, without the adjustment period of a receding hairline or widening bald spot; Elizabeth's clothes, clean but unironed, were alternately too big or too small; she didn't seem to know what size she was). They never made the kind of affectionate, scolding remarks that other people made to them all the time. All they offered was respect for each other's stunning haplessness. Out of consideration, they continued to act as if the other person had not destroyed the friendship.

"It's me," said Rachel.

"Are you all right?" Elizabeth would have driven all night for Rachel, offered her a kidney, shot her captors and coached her through labor, but she'd only called twice since Rachel came back from Kenya three years ago; Rachel didn't have time for a bad friend, and Elizabeth couldn't do any better.

"I'm fine." Rachel was always fine. "I thought you'd want to know Max is in the hospital. My hospital. Triple bypass. In his condition, that's not so good. Cabbage."

Rachel was in pediatric oncology now. She knew what was good and not so good, medically speaking.

"Oh my God. He's a cabbage?"

"No, listen to me. Coronary artery bypass graft surgery. That's just what they call it. What's new with you?"

Rachel's private name for Elizabeth, the name she uttered only in her head, was Slug. And when Rachel's heart was being trampled by the steel-capped boots of her latest snake-hipped, mean-hearted girlfriend, she thought it might not be so bad to be Slug, not terrific to be a burnout at twenty-four, but not so bad to be comfortably buried in a life of books and platonic affection.

"But he's okay? Is Greta with him? Who told you?"

"Sam Lieb had him in ninth grade, too. He saw his name on the patient list, sweetie. So I checked. Listen, I gotta go. He's not good but he's not dead. I heard they split up." There were loudspeaker voices in the background. *"Have* to go now. Bye, sweetie."

Elizabeth left Spivey's and drove the four hours to Great Neck. She had an extra-large, sturdy paper cup of coffee, two Heath bars, and forty bucks, which blocked the onset of really bad feelings. She parked behind what used to be Squire's Movie Theater, looking for Bee's Corseterie, and saw it was now a North Shore version of the Empress Josephine's silk-paneled dressing rooms. The new owners, who would not have hired the original Bee, served tea in china cups and concealed their cash register behind a large folding screen laminated with scenes from the *Rape of the Sabine Women*.

Elizabeth crept along the edges of the store, avoiding the four lion-maned salesgirls manning their stations in sheer silk blouses and long slit suede skirts, bits of fancy bra and flower-trimmed garter aggressively displayed above and below.

Did women really wear this stuff? Maybe he would have loved it, Elizabeth thought, fingering the chiffon-and-satin tap pants. I could have given him six years of leopard-skin bustiers and push-up bras and black silk stockings held up with black satin rosettes. I could have pleased him, I wasn't busy. And if I had, I could just let him die now, I wouldn't even have to send flowers.

The salesgirls were not unused to gloomy young women picking up silky items in despair, putting them aside, and picking them up again, eyeing red satin panties and hand-embroidered nightgowns with reluctant, embarrassed hope. Even the stupidest salesgirl knew that underwear, even underwear dotted with seed pearls and edged with slender pink ribbons through the inch-wide lace trim, didn't really make a difference. Still, they watched Elizabeth, and the youngest, newest salesgirl was determined to sell her something. She showed Elizabeth things young women wear to please young men, virginal gowns in transparent white cotton, strips of pink satin cut for small breasts and long, hard thighs.

"No," she said. "It's not what I'm looking for. My boyfriend's not this type." Elizabeth smiled, thinking of what type Max had been, and the salesgirl decided she'd been mistaken, that this was not another girl in love with the wrong guy.

"Okay, what type is he?"

"Conservative. Like a father." Like a father, if you wanted a life on talk shows.

"Your boyfriend is like my dad?" The salesgirl took a step back, clutching at the edge of a bleached pine cabinet filled with soft pastel undershirts, apparently taken off the backs of rich little girls.

"Sorry, I don't even know your father," Elizabeth said, very sorry that she was wasting Max's last hours on this blonde moron. "I just know—I just know this guy. Something outrageous, okay? Let's find something completely outrageous. Something to bring the dead back to life." The salesgirl was not happy, but she worked on commission. She helped Elizabeth find everything she wanted.

Elizabeth buttoned up her old raincoat in the hospital parking lot and went through reception. She passed two Candy Stripe girls, dark as cherrywood, with organza bows clustered high and bright atop their small sleek heads, like tribal headdresses from Woolworth's. The nurse at the station stepped in front of her, but Elizabeth said she was Max's niece and kept going. Pat O'Donnell was the daughter of Elizabeth's eighth-grade English teacher; she had her father's pre-ulcerous stomach and twenty years of nursing, and she knew that wasn't a niece, not with those heartsick eyes, but she didn't care. Might be interesting when the wife showed up.

Max lay in bed, his head propped up by two slippery hospital pillows, his hair a greasy spray of grey spikes. They had taken the tubes out of his nose but left two still winding down into his chest and another one connecting his left arm to a bulging, transparent drip bag. He looked like the Tin Woodsman, poorly patched and strapped together, wandering the cold world over for a heart. Elizabeth's own heart beat between her ears, blood pooling in her veins.

"You're here," Max whispered.

Tears floated on the inside-out red edges of his eyes, and the visit Elizabeth had imagined dissolved. She would not do a quick and funny strip for him, dropping one shoulder of her trenchcoat to reveal her black lace bra. The sight of her white skin and tight black garters would not raise him off the bed. Scented talc gleaming between her breasts and thighs would not steady his breathing. He was going to die because she had been selfish and stupid and childish. He was going to die because she hadn't answered his letters. I have to go right now, she thought.

Max's hands lay folded on his chest. *"Je ne regrette, je ne regrette, non, je ne regrette rien,"* he sang out hoarsely in cartoon French.

"Peter, this is Elizabeth. I need some sick leave or vacation, whatever. Time off."

"All right. Why?"

"My father's very sick. I think he's dying."

"Jesus. Your father? I'm sorry. Are you going to stay with him until . . . I mean, for a few weeks?"

"I don't know. I have to take care of him. I have to nurse him."

"Of course. You know, my mother died of cancer five years ago. Do what you have to do. I can hold the job for at least three months."

"Fine. Okay. I'll call you soon. Thanks." I should have gone out with you. I should be buying animal-shaped mugs and a butcher-block kitchen table, and I should be going in some other direction. I am not old enough for rubber sheets and bedsores and that smell which is as recognizable as reveille.

The backseat was layered with jeans and cotton underpants and all of Spivey's healthy-heart cookbooks and a shopping bag spilling new shampoo, new soap, two kinds of mouthwash and a sponge still in its natural loofah shape. Elizabeth had shopped like she was sending herself to camp. Camp Max, the special endless summer for wayward girls. She would be with him, in some small airless place, until he died or recovered or she killed him. She had a full tank of gas, she had her coffee, her candy, and enough cash. The radio was on and the windows were cracked open.

"Play 'Woolly Bully,' " said the tired Jersey voice. A housewife/mother voice, a three glasses of canned juice, three bowls of leftover Cheerios floating in thin, sweet milk by 7:25 a.m. voice. Screaming at the kids to remember their books, remember their notes, remember not to let the cat out. Kisses to remind them that she screams only because she loves them, wants them to succeed, wants them to be somebody. And then there is nobody home until three. A no-power, no-money voice.

"Okay," said the flat smirky deejay. "And do *you* have a woolly bully, ma'am?" Like he's behind her in the supermarket, laughing at her fat ass and curlers and the bent-in backs of her loafers.

"Oh yeah, honey. I did used to have one . . . but I divorced him."

She'd fooled them both, and the deejay laughed with Elizabeth, in the pleasure of acknowledging grace and steel where they hadn't seen it. Maybe he, like Elizabeth, imagined the caller as a mother, imagined the watery orange juice coming with the kind of mothering you never stop trying to get, or get away from.

"Lady, you can call me anytime."

"Likewise," the woman said. "So, put on my man, Sam the Sham," she said.

Elizabeth sang along. She began a list with her right hand.

In his hospital room, newspapers beginning to pile up by the bed, roses wilting on rubbery stems, Max made his offer.

"If you come stay with me for a little, you might get to watch me die. Or kill me at your leisure. Could you stick around?"

Elizabeth wheeled him to the car, sliding him into the backseat. Two orderlies stood by as if to help, but Elizabeth managed to bang Max's head against the car door and they didn't move.

"I want you to live, Max." She buckled his seat belt.

"Oh, sweetheart," he said, "I always try to give you what you want."

"No. You gave me what you wanted me to have. I'm not arguing with you. I want you to live."

"I don't think so, baby."

Elizabeth put her face an inch from Max's ear and spoke very softly and clearly.

"You better fucking live. If you don't make up your mind to live, I'm going to camp in your goddamned room and make sure you get intravenous nourishment and no painkiller. Okay? You better fucking live."

OH, DO NOT LET THE WORLD DEPART

▼

"Elizabeth, if you could get Max out of the place for a few hours, I could fix it up a bit."

"Mother, he hates to go out. Why can't you do what you're going to do while he's here?"

"I'm sorry, old thing. I simply can't."

Elizabeth understood that it wasn't a problem of logistics. Margaret could not make beauty in the presence of death. Elizabeth was only getting through the year by keeping her eyes closed. She hadn't looked in a mirror or even directly into Max's face for weeks. Why should Margaret step up to unnecessary pain?

"All right," Elizabeth said, "we'll go out to Mad Nan's Orchards and get some apples and feed the ducks. You know, I can't have him out for more than two and a half, three hours. Is that enough?"

"Fine. Call me when you're about to get your car."

"Mother, we don't need split-second timing for this. It's not a military maneuver, for Christ's sake."

"I am coming with three assistants and a van. I am going to do everything but paint, and I promise not to rearrange his books or records. I don't think Max would like to feel that I'm doing him a large favor, do you? I do think he can tolerate the idea that your mother is coming in to tidy things up a little, and to make her daughter's life more pleasant. All right?"

"All right. Jesus, Margaret, what a business. But thank you. What day?"

"Go for a spin on Thursday. That gives me four days to set things up and get these blighters moving."

"You do that, you get those blighters moving. Thank you." Elizabeth put down the phone. Was God obliged to close one big window in order to crack open this ridiculously tiny door?

Elizabeth used to stand in the kitchen of her parents' house, before Margaret had her downtown office, listening to her mother do business in that same happy, crisp, pugnacious voice. Four months ago, standing in Max's small, dirty kitchen, helping bag chicken breasts and turkeyburgers, her mother tried again.

She asked Elizabeth to talk to her husband's partner.

Elizabeth said, "Rachel"—now that Rachel was a doctor, Margaret no longer flinched when she was mentioned—"says Zoltow's very friendly with his female patients, friendly to the point of lawsuit." She slid two skinless chicken breasts onto a plate of Mrs. Dash and flipped them over.

"I'm sure Aaron could suggest someone else, then. A woman."

"Why would I go?"

"This is no way to live." Margaret waved her small hand around the three crowded rooms, the couch covered with blankets and Elizabeth's underwear, the dying plants, the cornucopia of medications spilled across the kitchen table.

"You're twenty-four. Why are you doing this? Do tell me. I would like to know."

"He's going to die, and he was there for me when I needed him. It's all right. It won't take that long."

Margaret nodded. Considering they'd never discussed Elizabeth's relationship with Max and that Margaret never allowed herself to think anything untoward about his constant and fatherly affection for her daughter, grateful that some paternal figure had kept his hand in, it was amazing how quickly she understood. "Nothing I can say, then? Trip to Europe, that sort of thing?"

Elizabeth shook her head and put her hand out to wipe crumbs off the counter. If she had known that her mother would never again have money to spare, she might have said yes and seen Paris.

Margaret caught her by the wrist. She blinked hard and did not cry and did not say, Is your life so terrible that you prefer this? She pulled Elizabeth's hand so close Elizabeth could feel her mother's warm breath on her palm. Margaret said, "You need a manicure," and pulled out a fresh bottle of Cherries in the Snow and an orange stick.

"Max, on Thursday my mother's coming to do a little housecleaning for us and hang a few pictures."

Max opened his eyes, his hair sticking up all over his head, like a great grey baby.

"Pictures? I can't wait. The entire history of the Empire, in jewel tones, right here in my boudoir. Tell her thanks."

"I did."

He closed his eyes again, tugging the comforter up over his

shoulders. When he was a little boy, he loved and imitated his stepfather's Irish tenor, the only sweet sound in a house of Mississippi ululation and breaking glass. " 'Twas on the Isle of Capri that I met her, something something a thin golden ring on her finger, 'twas good-bye on the Isle of Capri." The edge of the comforter poked his leaking right eye. He pulled it beneath his chin, pretended to sleep, and slept.

He woke up to find Elizabeth in his mother's pale blue velvet cloche and the pale blue wool peplum jacket she'd worn to demonstrate sobriety, and a withered white garter belt, with its rusty metal clasps swinging back and forth over Elizabeth's cotton panties. She wore her own basketball sneakers and white socks.

"Nice, huh?"

"Very. Interesting. Who are you?"

"Your mother? I couldn't get into the skirt. She must have been tiny."

"She was small. You're quite a bit taller. Bigger-boned, I'd say." He might be old, he might be dying, he might be every kind of fool, as his history demonstrated, but he had never told a woman she was fatter than another woman.

"I didn't know you had all these women's clothes. Fetish?" Elizabeth perched on the end of the couch.

"I guess. I never wanted to throw out all my mother's stuff, so I just threw it into my footlocker and took it with me. I don't think I've opened it in twenty years."

"How'd she die?"

"Cirrhosis. A very ugly way to die, I hear. I wasn't there."

Elizabeth put the back of her hand to her forehead, staggered around the couch, and collapsed in front of Max.

"I think I would have made a great Camille."

"Probably. Except for your robust good health. And your sneakers."

"I do love you. Was your mother kind of a party girl?"

"She liked a good time. She drank quite a bit, she had a lot of boyfriends between husbands. Or so it seemed to me, when I was a boy. Was there anything you wanted in there?"

Elizabeth pulled out a crumbling straw hat with chipped flocked velvet cherries on the brim.

"Hey, a come-fuck-me hat. There have to be shoes to match."

Max closed his eyes.

"Did I offend you? I'm sorry."

"You meant to offend me. This isn't much of a sport, sweetheart. Getting at me is shooting fish in a barrel."

"But if you really want the fish shot, what better arrangement?" She took off the cloche and the jacket and put on the hat. She took off her sneakers and socks. She put a wide elastic belt, a cluster of plastic cherries concealing the clasp, around her waist and kicked off her underpants.

"What do you want from me?" he said.

"I don't know. You don't have any money, what with Greta's house and Greta's shrink and Danny's darkroom and Marc's whatever. Why do we send Marc money?"

"Because he is getting a small design business off the ground in Lyons and he needs some start-up capital."

Elizabeth lay down on the floor beside the couch, her breasts brushing Max's fingertips. He pulled his hand up to his chest.

"Yeah. And because you feel guilty."

"And because I feel guilty."

"Don't you feel guilty toward me?"

"You know I do."

"This is a pretty funny apology, right? Come nurse me through this illness and let me try to make it up to you."

"I am sorry, Elizabeth. You were very kind to come take care of me. I know I loved you too much and too soon."

"The fuck you did." Elizabeth took his hand and pressed his palm over her breast. She sat up over him, her knees on either side of his chest.

"Touch me. Touch me now."

Max put his hands down, resting them on her cold heels.

"Now you don't want to?"

"I'm tired."

"You're scared."

"I'm scared because I don't know what you want. You can't want me."

"Why not? And if I don't really want you—I mean, you're right, I don't—maybe I want something from you."

"I'm really tired."

"What was your mother's name?"

"Louisa."

"Call me Louisa. Touch me there and call me Louisa."

Max didn't say no (he was not as scared as Elizabeth wanted him to be, but he was uncomfortable and he was angry; he's *dying,* for Christ's sake). He closed his eyes. Soft, matted hair brushed his nose and lips. He smelled her.

"Is this necessary?'

"It's hard to say. Was I necessary for you?"

"Oh, sweetheart, why don't you just leave? You don't have

to take care of me. Take the hat, take my passbook, and just go."

"I don't want to go. I want to stay here and be Louisa, that sweet little thing. Do you think having an alcoholic slut for a mother is what made you chase little girls?"

He wanted to say, You were not little. You were a young woman, and I was wrong, but you were not a little girl. He coughed very hard, bouncing Elizabeth on his chest.

She stood up and handed him a kleenex.

"Never mind," she said.

She left the cherry-trimmed hat on and dressed in her own clothes.

"I'm sorry, Pops."

"Forget it. I owe you."

Elizabeth looked away. "Yeah. Well. Can I keep the hat?"

On Thursday he was better. She found a bright red flannel shirt for him, and in his black overcoat and black beret he looked frail and chic, a French grandfather driving out to inspect the vineyards.

"Let's go feed the ducks, and we can pick up a couple of bags of apples. I'll make an apple pie."

"I never understood 'feeding the ducks.' Think about it. We buy stale bread so we can have the pleasure of feeding the ducks, who can't be hungry, since they're always being fed. And the store maintains the ducks so it can sell us stale bread. There are no more starving children? We have to come up with this arrangement so we can all play Marie Antoinette by the pond?"

He shut his eyes and Elizabeth kept driving, glad he was

talking. It was always a good sign when he had the energy to talk, no matter what he said. Even if it was about the stupid ducks.

Max thought, Why am I talking about this?

He sat on a bench while Elizabeth fed the ducks, and when she sprinkled breadcrumbs right at his feet, two fat black ducks came up, honking mildly. They were dirtier than she had imagined, something dark caked into the tiny holes on top of their beaks, algae and muck trailing their orange feet.

Max ignored them for a while, pulling his beret down over his eyes, covertly enjoying the sun on his shoulders and legs. The ducks pecked around the bench, and when he shuffled his feet a few times, they retreated and then came back, honking a little louder, pecking more aggressively.

"They must be female," he said, smiling. She didn't answer him except to bite down on an apple and chew it loudly. Max could no longer chew apples.

They drove home in silence, and when Max touched her thigh, Elizabeth looked down at the trembling loose skin and patted his hand. There's no point in being mad, she thought. There's not enough time. I could yell at him and then he'd keel over and the last thing I would have said would be, Don't be an asshole, Max.

That's how you know you're dying, Max thought. I could burn her clothes, shit in the kitchen, wave my dick at the goddamned ducks, and she'd just smile and pat my hand.

Max's place was tidier, piles consolidated and concealed, the air filled with motes of lemon furniture polish, ten pink roses as open as bowls, but it was not transformed. Elizabeth was glad she hadn't mentioned Margaret's true and apparently grandiose intentions. Her mother had failed; it still smelled like seeping death.

"Nice roses your mother left. Nice vacuuming. Thank her for me."

"Maybe you could. When I call. TV?" Elizabeth steadied Max on her hip, pulled off his coat, and held him up with one hand while she reached out to clear the recliner and slide him down into it. She saw that the recliner was empty, in an alien, pristine, showroomlike state.

Max patted the cushions. "All right. I wonder where she put my stuff?" He shut his eyes. "How about those monks?" Yesterday *Family Feud* had monks versus nuns and Max laughed until he cried.

"Okay, you watch. I gotta go out now, just for a little while."

Elizabeth picked up her keys.

"Where are you going?"

"We need some stuff, Max. I'll be back in an hour."

"Don't do anything I wouldn't do."

CAN'T TURN YOU LOOSE

▼

She saw him from the diner window, coming around the corner from the parking lot, his jacket flapping over his high country behind. Suit, white shirt, red tie. Polished black loafers on his big country feet. More waist now, just a little bit of gut pressing against his belt. Big, easy comfort, a long velvet-sofa man. Still those long legs and arms, coming past the rotating dessert tower.

"Well, Liz Taube. Bless your heart, good to see you again," Huddie said, and put out his hand.

Elizabeth stared like it had turned from hand to snake as he spoke. "Bless my heart?"

Huddie slid into the booth and leaned forward.

"Elizabeth? Liz? You still go by Liz? I work in this town, I own a business here now. I have customers in here, Nikos and I are on the same delivery run. You have no goddamned idea. You never did. I am a model minority businessman. I am a family man, I give to the church, hell, I give to the synagogue. You want me to stick my tongue down your throat by way of hello? Bad enough you showed up in my store like the Ghost of Christmas Past."

"What are you so pissy about? It's been seven years and you're the one that's married, not me. You've got babies, I don't. Excuse me, I would have written when you were in Buttfuck, Alabama, but you didn't. And I didn't know you were back." Elizabeth looked down. "Running your father's store. Christ."

The waiter stood by the table, grinning at Huddie.

"Hey, George, how's it going?"

"Good, Hud. Going good now." He licked the tip of his pencil, willing to wait for twenty minutes if that was how long Huddie took. George worked two nights at week at Nassau Produce, Huddie's store, and Huddie paid for twenty-two English classes, something his cousin Nikos didn't give a good goddamn about. If Huddie Lester wanted to take his time about ordering coffee, and then take this angry, sort of pretty girl to the motel next door, that was fine with George Pascopolous. Huddie Lester was his man.

"Give us a few minutes, buddy."

"Okay, Hud, when you want me, you do like so." George raised one finger discreetly.

She would have kicked Huddie under the table if he hadn't made her feel that everyone in the diner was watching them, completely fascinated. All that time apart, and now together, and it was not the same, of course, and this conversation would do nothing for them.

His jacket cuff rode up on his sleeve, showing a half-circle of brown skin through the white shirt.

"Are we having a conversation?" Elizabeth ran her palm over the Formica, rolling sugar granules with her fingertips.

"No," he said. "Let's get out of here. Let's not run out of here, but let us, by all means, get the hell out of here."

Elizabeth drove blind to Wadsworth Park, and he followed, watching the oncoming cars for familiar faces, composing a businesslike, everyday expression. She didn't even look at him getting out of the car, just slammed the door and walked into the woods like an Indian widow. Huddie looked around the empty lot and called to her.

"How about a blanket?"

"I didn't come that prepared."

"To sit on. I'm wearing a suit. We could talk in the car."

"You're killing me, Huddie. Let's just go for a walk."

They went past the rays of gravel tossed up from the parking lot, past the soda cans, candy wrappers, hot dog bun plastic and aluminum foil clumps, bits of old and crumbling forest suspended in the gelling, bug-speckled light. Huddie caught a yellowing condom on the toe of his shiny loafer and kicked it toward the stream.

"I don't have that little problem anymore."

"Is that right?"

He loosened his tie with one hand, and she sighed.

"We're not talking," he said, and he laced his fingers through hers. They both looked down, caught by what always caught them, what captured them when Huddie put his hand on the bleacher in the high school gym, resting the side of his palm so close to her leg that they both felt the soft prickling of the tiny hairs on her thigh. The absolute aesthetic harmony of their skin flared up and then subsided, outshone by the infinite exploding light of what came next, a beauty living only in each other, separate from their attractive, everyday faces, from body parts they liked or didn't like, from the lives they would have. Only their mothers, at the first moment of seeing, had ever read their souls so plain on their faces.

"You saw the store's bigger now," he said. "You ought to check it out. That front porch is for coffee and pastry, and we've got this big mother dairy case."

"I'll come again when your father's not there. Unless he's changed."

"You've changed more than he has, and you haven't changed much."

"I have."

"Have not." He pulled up her hand and kissed it. "Have not, have not, have not. So there. What're you looking for?"

"A tree suitable for seductive leaning."

"Don't bother. Don't bother looking. There's no need."

The tiny black pits of his shaved beard, the leaf fragments in his black hair, his slightly chapped lips, with a dry whitish spot smack in the middle of the lower one, were all she saw. Huddie licked the dry spot and kissed her. He put his wet forehead to her collarbone, his nose pressed into her neck so that he could only breathe by opening his mouth and pulling back slightly. They heard the damp suck of his kiss and he felt Elizabeth's silent laugh, and pulled away entirely. Anything but her sweet, lovestruck voice saying his name would push him back to his right mind, where he did not want to be.

"Huddie. Hudd-eee," Elizabeth whispered.

"I did write to you. I wrote almost every day, for weeks. I never heard back. My aunt and uncle said—well, you know what kind of things they'd say. I wrote one time to Mrs. Hill. I called your mother one time, but I don't guess you got the message."

"Never. And I didn't get those letters, Hud. She died right after you were sent away. Oh, boy. Broken hearts all around. I never heard from you, about you, at all. A few times I skulked around the store, thinking your father might have softened up, that he'd give me your address or just drop a hint."

"I don't guess he did."

"No, not even close. He did say that you'd be going to Howard. But I wrote to Howard that fall and they'd never heard of you."

"Howard? Shit, I ended up at Michigan. You obviously did not watch college basketball."

"Not much. A few times. It made me cry and I didn't see you. Ridiculous," Elizabeth said, hooking her hands inside his belt, feeling him big and wide against her, exactly as she thought he'd be. "Closer."

Huddie felt her breasts through her T-shirt, pouring through his suit and shirt, dense liquid hearts at rest on his middle ribs. He wouldn't say a word now, wouldn't exhale, stared hard at his watch the way a person who's not where he's supposed to be does. He wanted to cross himself, like the boys from Fordham, all of whom, even the Jews, understood that the cross was to placate Fate, to demonstrate humility and helplessness when all your talent and practice were not enough to swing the odds in your favor. He unhooked her thumbs, turning her palms down when she brought them up to his mouth, smooth, round palms, curved like her thighs, spread wide for the kisses he very carefully, gathering his wits, doesn't give. He fished for his car keys and left his hands in his pockets.

"Maybe we didn't really want to. Maybe we wanted to keep it the way it was." He sighed. "Who knows. I'm sorry about Mrs. Hill. Let's go, lady. I gotta get back to the store. It's the end of delivery day. There'll be six feet of charcuterie and eggplant terrine all over the floor."

"What happened to the pigs' feet?"

"We still got 'em. In the soul section. And shrimp paste and rice noodles and biscotti and tapenade. We upscale now."

And she thought that if he could be sure of not being mocked, he would be pleased and only a little sorry that the dusty Coca-Cola cases and cakey cans of Ajax were gone.

They walked to the parking lot, unable to resist bumping into each other, closing their eyes in the pleasure of his hip against hers, as though there were not four layers of fabric between them and not even five seconds before he reached his car.

"Can I start shopping at your place?"

"Does old Max have gourmet tastes?"

"I do." She was not going to talk about Max now.

"You come anytime. I don't go in on Sundays."

"Sundays you go to church in the morning, and then it's family dinner with your father, who is probably just crazy about your wife, and then you shoot a little hoop with your boys."

"Don't make fun of my life."

"That was longing, not mockery. Or longing concealed by mockery."

"My son is only four years old, and my knees are too fucked up for me to play. My father is no nicer to June than he is to anybody else. Otherwise you're right on the money. And you're going to mess up those Sunday mornings now."

"How?"

"Because in church, when they hit those high notes, I will not only remember us in that little yellow bed and in these woods back then, I'm going to think of you right here and I am not going to be thinking like a churchgoing man."

"Good. Me neither."

"You neither. Still funny."

"I am. Was the bed yellow? I thought the walls were yellow. Little yellow flowers."

"I don't think so. I think the bed was yellow, the walls were no color." He could still see the rickety bed, could see the wall as it looked to him, before and after he banged his head against it, leaving oily spots he would touch later, touching himself, thinking of her beneath him, his own amazing country.

"All right. I'll think of you too, Huddie. Horace. I guess this means we're not going to be getting together."

"For what?"

"For coffee, for lunch, for a walk."

"You know if I see you in private I'm going to make love to you, and if I see you in public this is not going to be our little secret for very long. A blind man could see how much I love you. I gotta go, sweet." His voice rough on that last word, and inside Elizabeth bright red streamers snap open and billow out in six-foot-long celebration. Inside Huddie, there is a quiet pinging, the warning sound of a failed alarm.

"Okay. I'll see you. Let's just get into our cars and go. I love you too. What's your son's name?"

He shook his head painfully, walking away. "Larry. I know you do."

They started their cars simultaneously. Elizabeth left first, nosing past his nicer, newer car and shooting gravel onto his windshield.

Huddie's wires cross every which way now. Sight, smell, taste, and touch enfold one another. Wet is like sweet is like heat is the aching pulse, is salt caking. Her smell is the smell of the unwrapped ready-to-rot figs, and for a lost half hour he scrunches thin lilac tissue paper around their small purple asses, tilting their stems so each seamed bottom is turned to its most seductive side. Carrot fronds are her hair; the slick celadon crack of a broken honeydew is hers and tastes cool, then warm. He puts his lips flat against tomatoes, plums, peaches, and nectarines before stacking them, and they ripen too fast, with hard-to-sell dark spots where his saliva has gathered and seeped in. Marshmallows, not even of interest since early Boy Scouts, roll out of their bags, pull his fingers into their sweet dusty white middles, pull themselves up around his fingertips. Half a bag. Twenty-three marshmallows. His fingers are stiff, powdered white, and his throat is glued shut, but the sugar thickly coating his lips and the drying tug from the roof of his mouth to the root of his tongue is so like a past moment between them he has to sit down behind the un-shelved goods, head resting on the giant cans of juice, sticky hands hard over sticky mouth, and cry without making a sound.

*   *   *

Three weeks later, after two embarrassing and badly cho-
reographed visits to Nassau Produce, half hiding to watch
Huddie sell happy women olive oils they never thought they
wanted and milk that was twenty cents more than the supermarket's, Elizabeth was finally naked, sitting up to admire
the way Huddie undressed, laying his red tie on the seat of the
armchair, unbuttoning his white shirt, hanging it over the
chair back to avoid wrinkling, and then tugging hard on his
belt, stomach sucked in and released, in that way that men
don't mind and women feel terrible about, and pulling off
pants, briefs, and socks in one piece.

"When did you get so polished?"

He turned his head, reminding her that when he blushed
the tips of his ears burned red as if the sun set through them,
and like that she fell in love again. For the red-brown tips of
his ears.

"I can't stand standing around in my shorts and socks. Like
an idiot."

"No. You look beautiful."

"Well. Now, you give me some room here, Elizabeth."

Huddie splashed water over his face, drinking some from
his hands, and looking in the little mirror, he saw his skinny,
lovesick young self. He wondered if God was more likely to
forgive him if he told June she could go ahead with another
baby and then he could leave her when the youngest, not even
conceived, was finally off to college, or if he could save himself some time and tell June now that Larry was enough,
which would allow him to leave, not dishonorably, in only
fourteen years. He sprinkled Elizabeth's chest with cold water

and watched the white-blue skin of her breasts crowd up into tight pink waves around her nipples.

Fourteen years.

"Ohh, it's cold, you shit. Horace, you shit. If we weren't here, drinking motel water, what would you want?"

Huddie picked up his watch, checked, and put it down. "To drink? V8 juice, maybe grapefruit."

"And to eat?"

"Is this the *Glamour* Quiz for Lovers?" June loved magazine tests and tore them out to answer right before bed. Tests for love, for budget balancing, for keeping your temper, for managing your in-laws. He answered every question of every test honestly, waiting for the terrible truth to hit June as she sat propped up on three lace pillows, totting up the scores, waiting to be touched.

"I don't think I'll ever get to cook for you. Tell me."

"Right now? A real Caesar salad, lots of egg, homemade croutons, heavy on the garlic. Really green olive oil. I'd cover you with leaves and eat it right off you. You salad bowl, you." He pushed June out of his mind; this little bit of time with Elizabeth would be lost to him if he waited for June to take off on her own.

He lay down again, setting the watch face toward him, and brought June back, waiting in the kitchen. He put his face deep into Elizabeth and willed his wife always safe and far away.

Elizabeth bit the soft flesh above his narrow hips. Maybe, without either of them noticing, without doing harm to June or Larry, she could mark him.

"Huddie, you're going to be a fat old man, you know that?

You foodaholic. Look at that gleam in your eye, homemade croutons. We'll end up two big porkers together. 'Come closer, my darling, closer.' 'I'm trying, sweetheart, I'm trying.' "

Huddie smiled and was stricken, not wanting to say that he did worry about his weight and every time he looked at his father's gut pushing wide black diamonds between his shirt buttons, he promised not to sample the triple crème cheeses, not to kick June out of the kitchen anymore, not to let the Belgian-chocolate sales rep leave him a two-pound gift box every six weeks. And as he looked to change the subject, bee stings of pure happiness fired up the back of his neck and shoulders. She saw them together, together in a who-cares, fat and happy middle age. Horace and Elizabeth, rocking, creaking in contentment on the front porch of a house near no one they've ever known.

She laid her white hand in the middle of his chest, scarless, dark mahogany, nothing like Max's, as nothing in the room was like anyplace she'd been lately. No real harm could come to you in a motel room, it seemed. The minute you hit the road, picked up a phone, found out that you'd been found out, all hell might break loose, but right then, between the see-through towels and the stiff green blankets, you were held in the safe, silent wall of the unborn.

"I'm starting to like motels," Elizabeth said, sliding his watch under her pillow.

Huddie put his hand over hers and the watch back on the nightstand. "I hate them. Except for this." He sighed and put his head on her back, smoother than the sheet. "I wish I had another life, a whole second life, for us." He brushed his lips over her ass.

"You'd get tired of me."

"I wouldn't mind finding that out for myself."

"This way we can keep the romance. You know, years longer than other people."

He lifted his head and pulled the sheet up to his shoulders, unbearably tired, filled with thoughts of June and Larry and everything he would lose and everything he had lost just in this hour, and she slid her fingers down his neck, flicking sweat off his chest. Who had left such wide, milky pools on the bed?

"All right," Huddie said, patting the hand on his shoulder, keeping his face turned away, to not see her tears, to not have her see his.

When he rose to leave, after three false starts, there was no afternoon light left, just the chill blue-grey of winter dusk and the white Hollywood-style bathroom lights buzzing through it.

"You're leaving," she said.

"Leaving you?" One of her hairs would not come loose from his tongue, her earrings had left twin, intimate gouges on his cheeks, and these awkward things gave him as much pleasure as all the official great moments of his life put together.

"No. It only looks that way. I am right here." He put his hand between her breasts, and felt his palm sink by quarter inches, lodging far beneath the surface of her skin. "Here."

BENEATH WINGS OF LOVE ABIDE

▼

Huddie knew it would be a disaster.

"Max will be at physical therapy. I know his schedule, I'm taking him there and picking him up. Don't worry, just meet me on your break."

They were both tired of the motel. At first, when he couldn't have even five minutes of his hand on Elizabeth's naked stomach, an hour on a bed, any private bed, was all he would ever ask for in life. He knew that it would be no time at all before even two hours on the bed wasn't enough; it made his chest hurt, it made the motel impossibly sterile, a disgusting black hole that took in conversation and sentiment and memory and left sex between two people in a hurry, trying to act as though an afternoon was a life. He liked comfort, a glass of juice, a bathrobe, real pillows. He liked decency. Huddie didn't want to raise the issue of the motel's shortcomings. He couldn't afford an apartment, and when he talked about leaving June, he and Elizabeth both burst into tears.

"All right. You sure?"

"Huddie, of course I'm sure. I'm the one who drives him.

I'll drop him off at around one, run a few errands, and meet you at two. I'll go pick him up at three-thirty. Okay?"

Huddie listened closely at the door and heard nothing from inside. Elizabeth wasn't back yet. The apartment was as he imagined, like his dad's place, more or less. Old-man smell, bathroom nastiness, a little lingering cigarette smoke and Old Grand-Dad, which made it very much like his father's house. Huddie was standing next to a musty, overloaded coat tree, one of Max's hats falling toward him, when he heard a gluey, rumbling cough that was not Elizabeth's.

"Sweetheart? Could you come here?"

Between his impulse to laugh aloud at the farce his life was turning into and his jacket's entanglement with the coat tree, Huddie froze in the middle of the front hall.

"Liz? I don't—"

Max leaned through the bedroom doorway, losing his grip on his unzipped pants. Huddie remembered a stronger and bearded face from junior high school and looked away from the shining white ball of Mr. Stone's belly.

"Mr. Stone? Max? I'm a friend of Elizabeth's. She invited me over for a cup of coffee . . ."

"And gave you the key?"

"She thought she might be a little late, from taking you to the uh." Huddie couldn't remember, for the life of him, where Elizabeth had been taking Max.

Max slid down to the floor.

"Could you get me the blue pillbox, from my nightstand? And the water?"

Huddie brought Max his nitroglycerine and pressed Max's hand to the glass.

"Okay now. Are you okay?"

"I'm not sure. I had this pain before." Max put his fist to the middle of his chest, a gesture that would ensure him immediate examination in the emergency room. "And I took a nitro and it was better. And now it's back. And a few minutes ago my jaw and my elbows ached. But they're not hurting now, so that's good."

"That is good. Did you eat something spicy? You know, heartburn?"

"Chinese food." Max was embarrassed to talk about eating with his belly resting on his thighs, in front of this well-built boy.

"Golden Chopsticks?" It was the place nearest Max's apartment, the place Huddie would go for Empress Chicken, given his choice.

"Yeah. Ahh. It's not better."

"Let me call your doctor."

"If it's an infarction, he'll want me to go to the ER."

"I'll take you."

"You?"

"Horace Lester. Let's go."

Huddie left Elizabeth a note and put an overcoat on Max, who insisted on slowly buttoning his shirt and zipping his pants to hide his nearly tearful longing for his blue sweatpants and his soft, mothering sweatshirt.

Everything in the emergency room happened quickly and efficiently. Huddie decided to say he was Stone's son-in-law, which could be, and that way they'd let him take care of him, or sit with him, until they did whatever they did. He apologized mentally to June and her father.

There wasn't five minutes of sitting, and the triage nurse didn't give a fuck who Huddie was. Max slapped down an insurance card, put his fist to his chest again, and in ten minutes Huddie was cooling his heels in the waiting room, Max had an IV dripping into his veins, and they'd hooked two monitors to his chest. Two white doctors bumped into each other behind a pale green curtain, and after the EKG one of them stuck his head out and nodded to Huddie.

Finally, the fat doctor said, "Let's play it safe. It's not an emergency, you're okay." He raised his voice to reach the nurse back at the desk. "Let's just say a soft romey and follow up tomorrow."

The nurse nodded, typing slowly onto pink paper.

A tear ran from Max's eye into his ear.

"What's a soft romey?" Huddie asked, as any good son-in-law would.

"Sorry. It's just 'Rule out myocardial infarction.' I notified his doctor. We'll get him to his room in a little bit, as soon as we get things calmed down again."

A white, limp girl was carried in, blood streaming down her forearms, and Max and Huddie watched, slightly ashamed of their relieved curiosity, like people with a flat observing the eighteen-wheeler flipping over in front of them.

They leafed through magazines until the nurse, whose white uniform was now lightly red-speckled, came over with a pair of orderlies.

Huddie rose as they put Max on the stretcher.

"Subacute c.c.u. Room 146," the nurse said.

In the elevator, the black orderly and the white orderly checked out Huddie and Max. Their relationship is not obvious. They might be old white employer, young black employee. Possibly, the black man's the boss and the old white guy's been working for him for years, but the old man doesn't look like he's been able to work for years. They don't look like friends, like poker buddies. It does not occur to the orderlies that the men might be lovers, or family. Neither of them would like those possibilities.

Max saw the grey elevator walls, the distorted reflections in the dented steel ceiling, the green sheet, Horace's hand, his fingernails smooth honey-colored ovals, longer than Max's, and Max wondered if all black men wore their nails long; he'd never looked at any man's nails before. He put his hand on Huddie's wrist and squeezed it. The orderlies took this in too, looking at each other sideways and then straight ahead.

The nurse hung a long grey rectangle around Max's neck on a cheap cloth band and stuck two new wires into the tabs on his chest. She smiled at the doctor walking in, and he gave back a small smile beneath his big moustache, showing that it was a serious business—don't even hope otherwise—but they were in good, even excellent, hands. He was visibly intelligent, arrogant, not unkind, taller than average. Max and Huddie thought only one thing: black. Max thought, Good. It will make Horace Lester feel good, and furthermore, he's not a young man, he probably had to be smarter than everyone else to go to medical school and become a cardiologist back then.

Huddie knew it was stupid to be pleased, but he was, and inside he's six and the Alabama kitchenware Aunt Les brought with her flies past him as she calls out, after each pot, lid, and saucepan hits the back door, "Lift up the race, child! Lift *up* the race." She lived with them for only three years, his Great-aunt Lessie, and moved back home, saying Gus was doing fine, Huddie was doing fine, and the cold was killing her. She prayed conversationally and constantly: instructing, cajoling, informing, and flirting with the Lord. She prayed for Huddie to learn to wipe his feet, she prayed for justice for her people, she prayed for Gus's loan to come through, she prayed for Gus to find a wife to mother the boy, she prayed that God would see fit to change Gus's ways so that the woman's life would not be Hell on earth. She smoked a corncob pipe at night and made Huddie hold up her big silver-backed mirror on Sundays so she could pluck two grey hairs from her chin, dress her long hair, and take him to church. On the occasional Sunday, he's found himself sitting behind an old woman smelling of woodsmoke and Dixie Peach and felt time collapse like a paper tunnel.

The doctor finished examining Max and making notes. He nodded to Huddie, patted Max on the shoulder. He walked out with a small, stiff-wristed wave, like the Queen of England.

The nurse stayed behind for cleanup. "Any pain, any complaints, call. Otherwise, sweet dreams, Mr. Stone. And—"

"Jack Robinson. Son-in-law."

Max smiled. "We're just waiting for my daughter to get here. Are two visitors okay?"

"Until eight o'clock, two is fine. Take it easy."

* * *

"The lights on the mirror," Max said, "it's like one of Liberace's capes."

"I never saw him."

"He's on TV all the time. Campy crap. You never saw him? The rhinestones? The candelabra?" Why was he talking about this? "Like Little Richard without the falsetto. And Polish."

"What's the goddamned point of that?"

"All right. You don't have to stay. Is Elizabeth here?"

"Max, if she were here, you'd be seeing her. She'll be here soon."

"All right."

Huddie took Max's hand and Max let him, then pushed his hand further into Huddie's. If he's dying, he will die holding a hand that loves.

When Elizabeth came, Max was asleep, still holding Huddie's hand.

"My Christ, Huddie. I'm so sorry. You had to bring him here? Oh my fucking Christ, that must have been something. Go back to the store, go home." She was practically pushing him out the door, knowing what this could cost him. If he's late at the store, his assistant, a well-meaning girl who thinks Huddie walks on water, will begin calling around. Eventually, someone will call June and Huddie will have to say something credible that in no way contradicts anything that anyone might have already said. He kissed her. "Take care of him, baby."

"Don't worry. Get out of here."

Huddie waved to her and was gone. Elizabeth didn't want

Huddie showing concern and affection for Max. They weren't even supposed to exist in the same universe. She looked at Max, drawing slow, bubbling breaths through his various tubes. He didn't look that much worse than usual. All right, God, whatever you want. I don't give a shit if Max lives, actually. You want him, take him. I am not trying to keep him here. It's enough. He's not getting better, he's a self-absorbed pain in the ass. That smell, old socks, and lesions. He takes his meds whenever, he lies to me about it. Whatever this is, it's enough. He was a good father, God, he taught me to drive a stick-shift, he taught me whole chunks of Auden, he made me listen to every kind of music. If you could give us a little more time, we could get all this straightened out. What's it to you? You didn't take him then, when it might have seemed like a good idea, for my sake, you certainly don't need to take him now. Ignore us.

Max coughed in his sleep and Elizabeth leaned over him, holding the plastic cup and the bending straw.

"You're here," Max said.

"Don't worry, I'm here."

"I met the guy you're fucking. Very nice guy."

"Yeah."

"Too bad he's married."

"Yeah."

"Well, you could break up his marriage, too."

"Get some rest, Max." She smoothed the sheet around his shoulders.

"Okay, Elizabeth." It is funny, the way he says it. They rarely call each other by name. Sweetheart, honey, darling,

baby girl, *milacku* is what he calls her. She calls him Pops or
Grumpy or Buster.

She sat by his bed, flipping through a magazine left behind
by the previous occupant.

"Baby girl. Go home."

"I'll stay, it's okay."

"Go home. I'd rather be alone. Go, go."

"If I go now, I'll come back in the morning. We can have
breakfast together."

"Fine."

"I'll bring you the *Times*. Love you, Mr. Stone."

"I know you do. Love you, Miss Taube."

It was terrible to be sent home by Max, although Elizabeth
had no wish to spend more time in the hospital. Max looked
sick but not frighteningly so. But he'd rather be alone than be
with her, and although she didn't like to think about it, she'd
rather be with Max than be alone, and that was why she was
back in Great Neck in the first place.

The charge nurse called at four a.m., and Elizabeth went
back to the hospital. A young nurse stopped her in the hall before she got to Max. They wanted her to sign a dozen forms,
including permission to perform an autopsy and to make use
of his organs. She began to sign, and another nurse, the one
who called the apartment—her Queens accent identified
her—said, "You're the daughter, right?"

"Not legally, no."

"Awright. Is there a legal daughter? A legal anybody?"

"He has a wife, I mean, I don't know if they're divorced.
And he has three—two sons. They're grown. One of them
lives here. One of them's in France."

"So then, really, Miss Taube"—the nurse had been skimming the notes while Elizabeth stumbled over who she was not—"really, we need to call the wife. If they're divorced, we can call the son, or whoever. It's nothing against you, it's a next-of-kin thing."

And so it was. Greta came down with Danny, and in the early morning, in the tiny green waiting room, where they'd been sent like squabbling children to sort out their differences, Greta hugged her silently. Danny, for whose weekly father-son dinner Elizabeth vacated the apartment every Wednesday night, said, "Call me Dan," and stared at the floor. Elizabeth assumed he was thinking, He ruined his life for you? She smoothed down her bangs.

"I'm glad he didn't die alone. Oh, dearie, we both thank you," Greta said. Dan grunted.

"What do you want me to do?" Elizabeth asked. She preferred not to have to move her stuff to a motel at five a.m., but the request would not surprise her, would not even strike her as unfair.

"Perhaps you can put his things in order, in the apartment. Marc is flying in tomorrow. He's doing very well in Lyons now. Max must have told you. Well, Danny or I will call you about the, about the . . ." Greta waved her hands.

"All right. I'm so sorry. If I had realized you were still married, I would have told them to call you first."

"Don't be ridiculous, dearie."

The nurse came for Greta, who made the smallest wave, a tilt of one open hand, as if they had never embraced, as if they'd barely traded names and hospital facts in front of the coffee machine and had not much cared for each other's tone or outfit. Elizabeth put her hand over her mouth and walked slowly to the parking lot. The big list in her head was who she cannot call. She cannot call her mother, who will not be sorry anyway, she cannot call Huddie, she can call Rachel in London, but it hardly seems worth it to track her down through the maze of the London Hospital for Children, reaching out for Rachel over the bald heads of little cancer patients to tell her that someone she felt littered the planet was now dead. The easy list was clothing, books, records, kitchen stuff, furniture, plants, stereo system. She was determined to do a spectacular clean-up job.

Elizabeth parked in front of Nassau Produce, waiting for Huddie. He saw her sleeping in the front seat and was glad to see her, because this particular face, this being, with the long boy legs and the mole on her right shoulder blade, is his lifeblood. It's not a source of pleasure right at this moment, that is just how it *is*. He's fed up with her bad judgment, first the meeting in the apartment, causing him six kinds of grief since yesterday afternoon, and now, lying here in front of his store, not giving a damn that June might have dropped him off or that he might have brought Larry in for a croissant or that his early morning people, the walkers who came in for coffee and the widows who began their day buying breakfast fruit and stopped in before closing for a fancy frozen dinner, would see her sprawled across her front seat, obviously not giving a good goddamn that someone from his life, which she didn't seem even to take into consideration, might see her and wonder.

He banged on the hood of her car, making more noise than he intended.

Elizabeth jumped up, her hair wild, her glasses still on but not quite resting on her nose. Huddie wanted to calm her down and he wanted to slap some sense into her.

"Max died," she said, holding on to the steering wheel.

"I'm so sorry, sweetheart. Why don't you get out of the car? Come on in and wash up and I'll make us coffee." It was the kind thing to do, it was also the most convenient and the least likely to destroy his life, which seemed highly perishable and sweet and in need of immediate care. Elizabeth wasn't a weeper; it would probably be okay to set her up at the table near the back, even if other people came in.

Huddie filled two mugs with fresh coffee and put a pile of rugalach on a plate, although his impulse was to hand her a to-go cup and a muffin in a bag. He showed her the bathroom and hugged her before she closed the door. He said he was sorry about Max, and he *was* sorry about the old man, seemed like a sad end to a sad life, but the real issue was that Elizabeth was now free to leave and might require a reason to stay.

Sunday night, on the way home from the movies, Huddie's arm began to tremble under Larry's sleep-heavy head. June had lifted Larry's head with one hand and folded up her sweater to make a pillow for him. Elizabeth doesn't know how to do that. He can't see her lifting Larry's head so smoothly it seems to grow out of her fingers, can't see her traveling with a comfortable sweater, extra kleenex, Life Savers, and a Frog and Toad book scrunched into a big vinyl purse.

June has four capacious, indestructible tote bags, in black, brown, navy, and bone. She is embarrassed and proud, too, defiant about her bags, all just like her mama's pocketbooks, and when they window-shop, she looks sideways at tiny evening bags with thin, pointless straps, jewel-studded bouquets, playful minaudières, and she shakes her head. "Not for the mother of Larry." She doesn't say anything about what the wife of Horace should wear. He won't tell her, and she makes herself believe, whistling in the dark of love's signless neighborhood, that he does like her, must love her, as Larry's mother, and will then come upon her, and love her, as June.

She fell in love as he spun through Michigan, a hundred times handsomer than the other handsome boys, kinder than the other sports stars. Even girls he slept with only once had nothing bad to say about him. A big hello for everyone, putting his arm around every girl, including the plain and dull, as if it were a privilege and a pleasure, always making it clear that his singleness was not due to any shortcoming on their part, but entirely and only because he hadn't been ready. And each woman knew that if he'd been ready, it would have happened with her. He attended eighteen weddings in four states the summer after his senior year.

June's small circle barely overlapped his; her friends were Christian, future nurses and social workers and mothers, and they held themselves apart from the radical girls with wide Afros and new names and hoop earrings to their shoulders, and apart from the Black Power boys in tight jeans and berets, sexy and scary and wrong, and they held themselves apart from the white girls who were everywhere, Jewish girls with auburn Afros and little blue glasses on their long noses, Protestant girls with Breck-shampoo blonde hair, flat as silk to their skinny behinds, managing to apologize for that hair and still toss it around a room like stardust. If June had not moved to Boston, by chance and because her mother's best friend was director of a nursing program, she might have lost Huddie sooner. But she saw him play two games for the Celtics (her mother's best friend was a fan, had touched the smooth hands of JoJo White and wept during John Havlicek's last game), jumping to the very rim of the basket, above the heads of bigger men, and she saw him fall to the hardwood floor like wet laundry. She heard the snap before she saw him curl up, grey with pain, and although it broke her heart, she was reasonably sure he wouldn't play again.

She had a girlfriend hand-deliver a sympathetic and encouraging card to his hospital room. She wrote Huddie about her old boyfriend who broke his knee and went on to play three more seasons (in high school and badly, she did not write) and sent a batch of oatmeal-raisin cookies. After two weeks, she sent another batch of cookies to his apartment with a friendly, dignified note on her own stationery suggesting the name of a good physical therapist. Finally he had to thank her, and as sweetly as she could, she kept him on the phone until a visit seemed in order. She was maid, secretary, cheerleader, and rehab assistant. She did not presume to call herself girlfriend, and when the model types were around she faded, and when they stopped coming, when his contract was not renewed and the Phoenix Suns went back on their offer and the Italians sent only a case of Barbaresco and their condolences, she made spaghetti with Italian sausage and listened while Huddie talked about red wine and the kind of restaurant he'd like to run. She finished nursing school and they were still together. And he had not found his feet in real estate or insurance or franchises and he didn't sleep well or long. He never blamed anyone. June was happy to be pregnant, happy to be a pediatric nurse, happy to leave the terrible cold and terrible white people of Boston, happy to be handsome, kind Huddie Lester's wife. She willed him to be happy with her.

In some alternate universe, Huddie and Elizabeth would make love every day, without fear or hurry, and if he had to, he would lie about it to June until kingdom come, lie willingly and shamelessly, lie and feel lucky to have the opportunity. But in this precarious world, he will not leave June and he will not become a man who sees his son every other Saturday and sends a check. Will not. Will not be another successful black man leaving his fine, kind, bronze-skinned wife for a white woman. A crazy white woman, with no common sense, no prospects, less of a foothold in the world than he had. A woman who doesn't even see the thousand things he has taught himself to ignore, the thousand things June knows, without discussion. Elizabeth has split herself open for him without knowing who enters her, the hundreds he carries with him, right to the bed, how much he owes to people she cannot even imagine. Marry this educated white girl whose people have money and still move down. Unbelievable.

The early morning crowd came and went. In ten minutes Michelle and John would drive up, put on their aprons, and go about their business. And Michelle would look at them as a black woman does, and John would look at them as a black man does, and much as they liked him, much as they owed him for various kindnesses of the past two years, the air at work would shift and June would hear. Huddie put a note on the cash register—"Back by 8:15. John, Basket Hill produce in the back. Michelle, bag yesterday's bread for St. Vincent de Paul. Horace"—and drove Elizabeth to Wadsworth Park.

"We need to step back, sweetheart. Not step away, but step back. I think so."

Elizabeth picked up handfuls of wet leaves and let them drop.

"We could just go on like this."

"I can't. I can't go from this to my real life. I can't have this not be my real life."

"You love me so much we have to break up."

"Shit. Yes."

Elizabeth shook her head.

"How about you love me so much you leave June?"

Huddie shook his head.

"Well, I must be the dumbest woman in North America. I did not see this coming."

"Sweet. Elizabeth. You don't see things coming. You never did."

"I will. Someday I will see things coming and I will jump out of the way. And if I see you, I'll run in the opposite direction. And if you see me first, you should do the same, you gutless son of a bitch. Drive me to Max's."

They drove in silence, wet-faced, two shrinking loose piles in the corners of the front seat, Huddie steering with two shaking fingers, Elizabeth's head on her chest. She shut the car door carefully. Surely, at the edge of the curb, at the corner, at the blurred traffic light, at the crumbling stucco arch over the entrance to Max's building, surely at some stopping point one of them would see that it could go another way, that it must, but Elizabeth finds her key and Huddie speeds through the changing yellow light.

He worked longer hours and claimed insomnia. He fixed up his father's house and built a sandbox for Larry. He ate all day long, stashing macadamia nuts in the glove compartment, dried figs in his pocket, a box of shortbread beneath his desk. Elizabeth fell back on old habits, her own and Max's, to get through a time so bad it made her long for elementary school. She made her way, at a numbing, workaday pace, through Max's stockpile of hard liquor. Max had anticipated a long, slow, tedious dying, and he had not expected to stop drinking until he was at death's very door. There was a bedroom closet full of Scotch and cheap white wine and three bottles of bourbon, which Elizabeth was able to drink if she mixed it with coffee. She shoplifted cans of crabmeat and lobster bisque and paid for bread and bananas and paper plates. Every day she stole something useful, a box of paper clips, a dustpan, a six-pack of sponges, so she could put Max's things in order. Margaret called to read her the obituary, which mentioned Greta and the two boys and his long teaching career. It did not mention Elizabeth or Benjamin, and she was not invited to the funeral. No one called her about it, which seemed small of them, but she had no wish to go.

She packed and cleaned and hung outside the windows to wash them. At night she flipped through Max's journals with less interest than she expected and drank until her eyes closed. When she touched her face, it felt like oil over dust.

When Dan finally called, all Elizabeth had to do was shower and put on the set of clean clothes she'd left folded on top of Max's dresser for the last eight days. The sheets were washed and dried and put away, the drawers were empty, she'd never been there. She took Louisa's paste diamond earrings and cherry hat and left the stock certificates and passbooks in a daisy shape on Max's desk.

"What did my father tell you about me? Did he tell you what a strange boy I was? What a strange boy I am?"

"No. He loved you very much, he was very proud of you."

"He didn't know fuck-all about me."

"I didn't say he understood you or your photographs. I said he loved you and he was proud of you. He supported you all those years, in every way, and he gave you everything he could. He paid for college, he gave you money to go to Mexico. Did he have to *understand* too? I used to let you stay up until midnight, remember? I'm the person who sat with you when you had those nightmares, when you were little, remember? I don't think you have to swear at me."

"You sat up with Benjie. You put Marc and me to bed early. Marc thought you were a bitch. He did a whole comic strip about you. 'Betty Bitch.' I loved you so much then. I never even fucking saw you again. You left me, you left him, and that was it. When you lay down on the bed next to me—my nightmares weren't that bad, by the way, I just wanted you beside me—I used to look down your shirt. You finally started wearing a bra, I see. I wasn't so little. I just didn't hit puberty until I was fifteen. You were gone by then. Did you babysit us just so you and my father could be together?"

"That's actually a very funny question. No. Max thought I was crazy. I wanted to be just the babysitter, a normal girl. So

I wouldn't let him touch me, kiss me good night, nothing. Not so much as a squeeze on the knee. More happened on my other babysitting jobs."

"But he could fuck you all the other times, go down on you all night long while my mother was in Europe, visiting what was left of her family."

She sat down in Max's recliner. "Yes. You want to hear 'yes'? Yes."

He unbuttoned his shirt. His skin was just like it was when he was little, white-gold over big blue veins snaking down his smooth shoulders and chest. The skin of martyred boy saints, luminous and sheer. His hands were just like Max's used to be, long and square, with thick fingers. No stiffening grey tape over hands like old fruit, no bloody skin puddling around the entry point of the IV drip. Elizabeth had watched him sleep a dozen times, flat on his back in his nightshirt and his little white underpants, his briefs sliding down below his smooth stomach. His little penis and his pointy little hipbones made a triangle in his underpants, and she would watch for a few minutes as the little tent got bigger and then shifted away, until it was no different from looking at a girl.

" 'Going down on her is like licking honey off the back of the tiniest, rose-enameled demitasse spoon. Not a spoon, no spoon has that softness, that thick, soft, bite-me quality.' "

Elizabeth got up. "You read his journals."

"Of course, whenever I could. I wanted to know, just like you did. I wanted to know what he thought of me, what happened between the two of you, what happened with my mother. You two had a very weird relationship."

She stood so close to him she could feel his breath on her

forehead. He backed up. "Yeah, we did," Elizabeth said. "We had a very weird relationship for a very long time. He sort of ruined my life and I loved him very much and now he's dead, and frankly, that's okay. He's not in pain anymore, and I am, so there you go. I took pretty good care of him, I think, and I would not have been able to go on doing that for another year or another ten years or even another month. And we were lucky enough to have an ending that worked out much better than the rest of our relationship, and that's all I want to tell you. That's it."

"I'm sorry. You don't have to go tonight if you don't want to." He put his hand to her wet face. Elizabeth turned away.

"Well, I do, actually. But not for a few minutes, Snurfel."

"You remember that game."

"You also had pretty weird relationships. Do you remember the time you hid all of your mother's paints?"

He had hidden Greta's paints to make her stop creating surreal canvases of ghostly Nazi uniforms and slaughtered animals, severed heads scattered in the wheat fields, torn grey uniforms flung into wormy apple trees. Greta asked him if he'd seen her paints, and when he shook his head, afraid to say the lie, she walked three miles into town with him and bought fifteen fat new tubes for herself and a leather-handled cherry-wood box of twelve oil paints for him, with three soft brushes, its own smooth wood palette, and its own pretty little metal cup for turpentine. It was not what he wanted or needed, and he left it in the yard underneath a madder blue hydrangea, wet and warping through the whole of fall and winter.

Elizabeth made tea for them both and found Christmas cookies in an unopened tin. They remembered the make-believe game: Congo Banana and Little Chimp and Farfel, Furfel, and Snurfel, a family in which the father roared at the mother, the mother bit the babies, and the babies burned down the hut. Elizabeth was only allowed to be They, the force that moved the dolls (a Gumby, three small bears, and a G.I. Joe, which served as Congo Banana, the father) and rearranged furniture during scene changes.

They unpacked Max's records of Gregorian chants and Yemenite rock and roll and plugged in the stereo. They poured a little rum into their cups and then poured some more into the teapot.

"You take off your shirt," he said.

Elizabeth sighed and unbuttoned her shirt, thinking, This cannot be what he really wants, my hair's sticking up all over the place, this bra is unraveling, I smell like Lysol.

" 'I love to kiss her breasts. They have the same faint, gold down that you see on those gorgeous Seattle peaches. I hope I die with that velvet feel on my lips.' "

Elizabeth lay down on the floor, and Dan lay down beside her, the two of them closing their eyes.

"I wished he would die, sometimes. He caused my mother such pain." Dan laughed. "It was a two-way street, I guess. Is this okay?" he asked, one hand skimming over the places Max wrote about.

"Okay," Elizabeth said. "Yes."

Like tired babies, like collapsing balloons, they lay flip-flopped over each other, ignoring belt buckles digging into soft parts, ignoring the impulse toward sex that death brings out in people even more ill-suited than Dan and Elizabeth.

"Good night, you banana," Elizabeth said, folding up the

rug corner with his shirt to make a pillow for him.

"Good night, Lizzie. *Dobrounuts*. Thank you." He threw both arms over the shirt and the rug and closed his eyes.

Elizabeth kissed his forehead and took her bag out to the car. She came back for her jacket and put the apartment keys on the table and kissed him again, as if he were the Max she'd never met.

PART III

THE GREATEST OF THESE IS LOVE
▼

I know he's on the road. I feel him coming. I don't know when or why or what he'll expect my house to be. Funny enough to me that it's my house. That I own a house. Safely in the middle of the middle block, and the only thing that stands out is the wild army of tulip trees in the front yard. I never even thought about making this place interesting. It is comfortable, it is normal; it lies on the lower end of the neighborhood spectrum, true, but in a way that arouses tolerance, not disgust. I am not like the Gilroys, who don't water, and I am not like the Boenches, who have built a three-car garage and subtly but definitely offend in the other direction.

When he gets here, he'll try to figure out which house is mine (the letters have fallen off the mailbox), and as he is driving slowly by, he'll see Max on the lawn, turning cartwheels.

Huddie sits in his car, wondering where to park, and sees a young white boy on the lawn turning cartwheels, and he knows—the hair, something in the face—the boy is Elizabeth's. And queer. He can see the boy's queerness from two houses down. Jesus, he thinks, just get him a tutu. Huddie reaches for the bouquet, studying him. Once he's with Elizabeth, been invited into her house, he'll have to pretend not to see the narrow, puffed chest and the thin shivery shoulders. Boy life will be a horror for this child, and some man will have to take up for him. A mother will not be enough. You'd have to make him a faggot to reckon with, a queer you'd think twice about bothering, even on a hot, dull evening.

Huddie climbs out of the car slowly, flowers first, wishing he weighed fifty pounds less, feeling like a beached black whale in the eyes of this very white, very thin kid. The boy averts his eyes from Huddie and goes right to the flowers, apparently approving. Huddie would throw them away if the boy hadn't seen them already; how could he have brought something so obvious, so desperate? He knows enough about wine to have chosen something impressive. One red, one white, maybe two big-bowled glasses. He could have brought her interesting cheeses from local farms, seven different kinds of crackers nestled on damask in one of the big willow baskets he now charges fifty dollars for. These flowers are bleeding away their purple foolishness, wetting the pretty tissue, the bottom of it limp, falling away in his hand.

The huge bouquet of lilac and purple irises is visible all the way from my living room window. There must be four dozen flowers in all that pink tissue. It's the Kilimanjaro of bouquets. He's studying my child. Max bangs on the window for my attention, and when our eyes meet, he stretches up his skinny arms and puffs out his chest. Even as he goes into his backward walkover, he has the sweet obsessive look of a leaping cat, and a cat's light slant eyes. His legs spring out supple and wide as a wishbone beneath baggy grey shorts that slide up his smooth thighs, revealing his underwear. He wears inconspicuous boy clothes—a dirty T-shirt, ratty sneakers on bare dirty legs—but they're useless as disguise when he's shrugging his shoulders or tossing his straight blond hair back like a starlet. He is the perfect thing in my life, and I would like to get him some adequate protection. I wouldn't flash gold jewelry in the bad part of town and I wouldn't send this child into the world without a man. I am not only not enough, I think I am trouble.

I see Max watching Huddie as he gets out of the car. He still moves easily, but he needs more room. Much more room, he's a big man after fifteen years, almost as wide as his father and taller than I remember. Huddie puts his legs out of the car carefully, scanning the street. I have half fallen for a dozen black men over the years for no other reason than that they exit their cars the way he does, the slow, self-possessed unfolding of a big man to his full size, making clear that he will not be threatened, that there is nothing to fear. And if there is, if you insist, he will reluctantly give you the trouble you're looking for, kick your sorry ass, and go on about his business. It says Don't. Fuck. With. Me. and it is the required daily grace under pressure of a black man in a white place, and although it must exhaust him, it moves me, and although I would think that understanding its ugly root would make excitement impossible, it excites me.

He must look enormous to Max. I don't think he's ever seen anyone so big in every direction, coming wide and high and black-oak solid into his speculative, pale green gaze.

I think Max knows exactly which house Huddie is looking

for, knows why he's come, knows that this is the man who has come for his mother. I want to think this. I'm beat. I have been explaining single motherhood and conception and marriage and homosexuality and commitment to Max since before he could listen, and I am tired of saying things clearly and reasonably in hopes of warding off trauma. Mad giggling is Max's response to my sensible, sensitive explanations, and right beneath that, furious disbelief. When he is most angry and disbelieving, he sticks out his tongue and pulls down his lower lids, making faces so ugly and not-funny that it's clear his only wish is to make me stop telling these ridiculous and frightening lies. He finds most adult men terrifying beasts, especially the fathers of the little girls he plays with, and he does not believe, for one minute, that there are women who like to live with them or that pairs of men make happy, healthy lives (I say the three words together always, banishing all disease, grief, and loneliness) in the worlds of Provincetown and San Francisco, and certainly not that I actually parted my legs and let a man put his penis into my vagina. He prefers to believe that I lay very close to, was perhaps sandwiched between, his idols, Mr. Rogers and Peter Pan; their united sperm would in fact explain why I have a child like Max.

"Hi," Huddie says. I spy behind the curtains. Mothers have divine dispensation for listening in, sheet-reading, dream interpretation, and interrogation. I don't say we should, just that we do. I do. How else can we know what to do, whom to save, where to go when they don't come home? The amorality of my childhood, my shoplifting and wholesale lying, is nothing to what I do, and am prepared to do, every single day for this boy.

Make my son cry? I'll hunt you down on the playground and pull your miserable heart right out of your weaselly little chest, and after dropping off the sympathy casserole for your mother, I'll stop by the classroom to remind Mrs. Miller that there is now a space in the Bluejay reading group and Max really *is* ready to move up. I have made a whole life for us, and although I sometimes feel like those intelligent felons, escaping through the prison laundry truck to practice small-town medicine, well and attentively, for twenty years before the Feds show up, it is a life that makes sense to me. I can do this job better than any other. I am happy every morning and I am sad only late at night.

Max stands on his hands, and his arms begin shaking.

"How long can you do that?" Huddie asks. When we knew each other and Larry was four or five, he timed and measured and reported every athletic moment in the boy's life. Fifty-six seconds underwater. Nine flights of stairs in two minutes. Two goals in the last quarter.

"I don't know. You can time me." Max rubs his arms and flings himself up into the air again, hands pressing hard on the grass as he turns a few more showy, foot-waggling cartwheels that end in round-offs of the kind the little ponytailed professionals do as they come off the beam. His feet slam the ground, and he raises his arms above his head for another handstand. I hope he hears a stadium crowd screaming his name, wild with love and admiration.

I come outside, standing still long enough for the afternoon sun to warm the tops of my bare feet, long enough to realize I haven't changed my clothes. Maybe he will think this is ironic on my part, that I have dressed "as" something, something like a housewife, although he can't think I've bought a house and supported this child by staying home and dusting. Huddie won't disappoint Max by taking his eye off the sweeping second hand, so instead of a solemn handshake or an affectionate embrace or even a sweetly tentative palm on the shoulder, instead of anything that we have a right to expect after fifteen years, we get another minute or two of oblique suspense and parental obligation. Huddie's smiling, keeping his eye on the watch. I smile at Max's pointed, quivering feet, at Huddie's handsome, broad chest and his hands, which are graceful, even shapely, and wide as catcher's mitts, and a familiar thorny stream washes under my lids.

I know my face is longer and his is wider, bulldog-wide through the temples, with darker-edged folds beginning above his eyebrows. We both have grey, but he can't see mine because I colored it yesterday, and despite its sprightly, mendacious auburn, I spent an hour crying and wiping dark, intractable spots off my forehead and off the tips of my ears. Although I no longer looked as old and time-speckled, I didn't exactly look like me. Already concealed, I was tempted to go for broke and did, with mascara and silver hoop earrings and clean, intact underpants. Actually, new underpants.

"Okay, Max. Maximus. Get upright."

"Eighteen seconds. That's good." Huddie's hand covers Max's to the middle of his damp little arm. "I'm Horace Lester, old friend of your mother's."

"I'm Max. I'm eight. I'm small for my age, but I'm eight."

"Good to meet you."

I can hear Huddie thinking, Small, yeah. Small and then some. Just keep him out of *my* son's locker room. My own thoughts about Max run so protective and so cruel I don't give Huddie time to ask even the normal visiting grown-up questions. Maxie pulls his hand out, not rudely, and backs up for a series of handsprings. Huddie gives me the flowers, without ceremony, and I look inside for a vase to suit them, knowing I don't have any. My impulses of the last eight years have not been toward the house beautiful. My mother had vases for every kind of bouquet and arrangement, and she had ideas about what suited which: glazed terracotta for wildflowers, tall crystal for tulips and snapdragons, short crystal for bunches of zinnias. I have a large peanut butter jar for most of Huddie's bouquet and a spaghetti sauce jar for the rest. I long, as I have not once longed in all these downwardly mobile years, for a tall column of etched glass, for a handsome, wide-mouthed ginger jar. I wanted safety and quiet and books and have them, but now it feels less like simplicity or even the successful marshaling of extremely limited resources, and more like the road show of *Grapes of Wrath*. My teeth ache with shame. I want those vases. I want a big walnut table and Portuguese pottery. I want pretty things right now, and I want him to come in and see my inviting, welcoming home and long to be in it. I want a house of layered charm, from the shining wooden floors to the witty, incidental watercolors, not a couch whose surface is a mix of Astroturf weave and backyard crust. I want a house where things have form as well as function, where not every surface says make do and don't notice. I wipe the Formica table (ten dollars for the table and three chairs at a tag sale) and put the jars on the counter. I cannot believe that I don't own placemats.

Back outside, watching Max, standing so close to Huddie I

smell his wheaty, wild onion scent and feel the faint heat of his back and chest, I see my mother, propped up on her twin bed, in her small, spare apartment (most of her money gone with her only really bad mistake, a light-fingered, slew-footed boyfriend after Aaron Price died), saying in her most fluting and therefore most furious voice, "Of course, one makes a virtue of necessity, my dear. What else? At least we have the pleasure of fooling others." And she made herself over once more, into an admirer of the simple life, a Zen devotee, as she had made herself domestically suburban, and then professionally successful, and then a desirable woman of leisure and a certain age, when not one of these things spoke to her own wishes; she made herself pure and died between rough cotton sheets, her bald head on a pillow as harsh as a bag of rice. I squeeze my eyes and conjure the kindest, most virtuous portrait of myself: a sensible, literate woman of limited income, a devoted mother who's chosen time with her child over professional advancement and a safe neighborhood over service for eight. Please see that.

The sky is the bright unchanging dusk of summer night; the tulip trees darken and fill until suddenly there is no light at all coming through them. We have to go in, both of us as reluctant as Max, as if there are no mosquitoes, as if tomorrow will be no good, as if this, this handspring, the one he can't do in the velvety dark, is the one that must be done tonight.

The porch light sends Max's shadow across Huddie's light grey pants and Huddie's across my porch steps, onto my feet, and I think, It will be all right if I die tonight. After I touch him.

I hand Huddie a glass of cheap wine and direct him to a

quiet corner. While the kitchen is briefly under siege, I am the
commander in chief. I hold on to the last two inches of Max's
T-shirt and clean his ears and his neck, wiping off the three
dripping circles of boy-colored stucco beading his lily throat.
My shoulder's pressing the phone to my ear so I can promise
brownies for the Great Gator bake sale. (Great Gator is the
mascot of Max's elementary school, and his snarky, omnivo-
rous green presence is felt almost every week, since I in fact
moved here, to this nothing-special house I can barely afford,
because the school takes its mascot and its honor classes and
its after-school program so seriously. Yes, two trays of brownies, and don't make me mad by explaining that the kids prefer
homemade.) I shake zucchini, peppers and garlic in my oldest, favorite pan, so old scorch marks tiger-stripe the original
fifties-kitchen yellow. I know how I look, moving around the
kitchen in double time. It impresses and intimidates men who
want to be married. Also young single women. Married men,
with children (who show up periodically with bottles of wine
when our children have all gone to bed), don't care for it
much, since they see it at home all the time. It must be as
charming as leg hairs in the sink. And other mothers, the few
who have been in my home (a six-week friendship between
Max and the boy across the street; the neighborhood cancer
drive; the new neighbor), don't watch, don't think about it,
they don't even put down their wineglasses as they set the table
for me. They have all they can stand of their own necessary,
gratifying agitation, whirling through their own kitchens like
dervishes, scattering silverware and instructions and things to
be defrosted and things to be frozen, feeling absolutely necessary to every movement and every living thing.

* * *

Huddie finishes his glass, a thin, sugary white, and wishes again that he'd brought decent wine instead of those irises, now bending in half over the jars she's jammed them into. He puts a splinter of raw zucchini in his mouth and thinks of all the great meals he's made, all the hot, oily bits, melting disks of fat and sugar he's needed, to fill the space this short-tempered, weary woman left in him. Reaching for a fallen bottle of oregano, Elizabeth looks for a moment like June's white twin. Muscular women, one plush layer over a wide back and hard legs striding until the last march. Bobcat wrestlers, point guards, piano-moving women. Stand in their way and *be* moved, fool. Elizabeth straightens up. He has misremembered. She has five inches on June and none of her broad curves. But her girl-arrow shape widens now to a protective, unshakable stance just like June's, what love light there is shines only on their children's faces. Except something else crosses Elizabeth's face, opening and closing like a night rose. Her young face was two curved blades pointing to her square chin. Now there are soft velvet pleats along the jaw, a row of faint, sweet ridges he would like to touch as she lowers her head to check the vegetables. And as she bends over awkwardly to get a roasting pan for the little pink potatoes, not the practiced kneel of stewardesses and office ladies, all of whom know that men are always looking, Elizabeth bends her knees only a little and her ass juts out, hips low and wide, her waist calling for his hands, her ass pressing toward him in those old jeans with their white, pulling seams, and Huddie thinks that it was for this that he has lived so long. Lead me on to that light, Lord, lead me home.

*   *   *

"Sylvan," Max says after dinner, looking out at the yard, his legs stretched out from the couch to the coffee table, like Huddie's.

Huddie says nothing. Don't mock my child. Do not say "Sylvan?" like it's a sissy ten-dollar word. Do not say "You mean green?" like no real boy would say anything else. Say "You are a faggot, Max." And then I'll have to kill you, and my grieving, delicate boy will be shuffled from foster home to foster home, bullied by no-neck monsters, made to wear polyester clothes that will so madden him he'll run away at the age of fourteen—I can see him with blond down on his cheeks, little gosling tufts—and find himself go-go dancing in some big-city Combat Zone, stripping down to a sequined, bulging G-string to the strains of "Over the Rainbow" for sticky dollar bills from the hands of vile middle-aged men.

"Yeah, it is," Horace says.

"I love that," Max says.

"Yeah."

Huddie and Max sit on Max's bed. This is the beautiful room in my house. I held his little biscuit feet in my hands, in this room. And beneath those feet, my hands, which I had always admired for their smoothness, were as worn and rough as cedar bark. Ivory angel feet, with opal nails and satin soles. And my hands became his steps, my body his playground, and my whole past was dissolved into his immediate, inescapable *now*.

Max's bedroom walls are the elegant Parisian yellow my mother would have chosen, and the ivy stencils from floor to ceiling are also her kind of thing. It was my last unnecessary effort. We came home to this house and three barely furnished rooms and nine drifting, cocooned, and expensive months together. We lived in baby time, where if you've cleaned up the spilled talcum and gotten to and from the grocery store, you've had a *day*. I had no other life than Maxie's, and I could neither remember nor imagine one. A leisurely shower elated me. Tiny red sneakers on sale with matching red and white teddy-bear print socks thrilled me. Burned toast and puddles of zwieback filled the kitchen and I swept it all into the garbage whenever I had the energy. I saw people only as they saw Max, and so I was inclined to love them. My father sent several thoughtful but not excessive checks and a stuffed pink panda, so gaudy and lush I could only assume his new wife had picked it out. He did not send a ticket to Oregon, and I thought, He's seventy, he's got a fifty-year-old wife with two college-age kids, her elderly, forgetful mother lives with them, fair enough. Some people are your family no matter when you find them, and some people are not, even if you are laid, still wet and crumpled, in their arms. Sol had found the right family, finally, including a stepdaughter who screamed good-naturedly at him in the background, "Sol, Jesus fucking Christ, I'm waiting for a call, you know. Tell her Max is gorgeous, send her a crazy big check, and lemme talk to Kenny before the concert's sold out." I thought that when she dropped out of college and got tired of Kenny, I might persuade her to babysit Max. And me.

The apostle spoons went on the shelf over the changing table, and Max had every bath in the company of gospel greats. Greta found me and sent a painting of crows and snakes, which I put back in its crate and hid in the attic, beneath zipperless luggage and winter clothes. My mother was dead but showed up in dreams so hilarious and realistic I had to believe that her soul had migrated to my subconscious, from which it was now directing late-night cinema. In my dreams, we discussed breast and bottle feeding, the right age for solids, wheat allergies, and the ways in which Max was clearly superior to the little white lumps we'd bubbled next to at the YMCA Tot Swim. We agreed on everything, and when I wavered in my own convictions, my mother, in the pale, pale lilac charmeuse evening dress she wore when I was nine, assembled experts from Anna Freud to Oscar Wilde to reassure me.

Huddie puts his hand out to smooth Max's hair, spread out on the pillow. He has done this a thousand times, and always with pleasure, but not to hair like this.

"I go to Hebrew School. I'm in Hey. Last year, I was in Daleth. That's practically babies. We carpool with the Shwartzes and the Manellis. I hate her. She's really, you know, she stinks."

Huddie gives the blanket a tug and sits down, moving two black velour gorillas (one with red bow tie, one with peelable banana in paw) to the foot of the bed. In the language of parents and children, Max knows this means his time is almost up; Huddie anticipates the last sleep-defying whoosh of conversation, Max's long day swirling out in a cloud of words and coded feeling.

"Are you Jewish?"

"No, I'm not. I go to church from time to time." The ten years he was a deacon are a flat dream, a life built from the outside in: deacon, Chamber of Commerce president, New York Produce's Man of the Year, County Youth Basketball coach, good father, good husband, as far as the job went.

"Some people convert." Max says this into the foot of an eyeless Raggedy Andy doll. "Our snack lady was born Catholic."

"Uh-uh. There will be no conversion, Mister Max. I think being Jewish is great for you and your mom. But I'm not Jewish."

"I don't think it really hurts that much," Max insists. Huddie winces and wonders if that is really Max's point, to say "I know you have one. I have one, too. And we are not alike and if I could I'd get the men who are like me to cut yours off." Max shows what Huddie recognizes as a full-court-press smile: both dimples and the upper lip slightly lifted to reveal the shining white incisors. He is not without weapons, after all. Max raises his arm, and for an insane minute Huddie thinks Max will rest his small hand on Huddie's groin. The boy takes a headless Ken from under his blanket and tosses it into the garbage.

"Three points. Good night, little man," Huddie says.

"Good night."

"You can call me Huddie."

"Huddie. You can call me Max."

"Good night, Max."

"Good night, Huddie. Good night, sleep tight, don't let the bedbugs bite, ducky!" This last is yelled like a football cheer.

Huddie turns out the lights, smiling, and wonders who the

father is, who's been fucking her for the last fifteen years. Apparently, the wish to possess that hit him when he saw the undersides of her white thighs long and harshly flattened out against the oak bleachers has not gone. For the last fifteen years he's believed he was not a jealous man and it turns out he just didn't remember.

Max's sound sleep makes us nervous. We shift around on the couch until we are far enough apart to look directly at one another. Huddie's stomach presses over his belt in a powerful, endearing slope, and his arms are as big around as small barrels, filling his shirtsleeves. If I cut him, he will open brown, red, pink, down to white bone, small petals of blood rising on his skin. But he puts his arm on the back of the couch, and now I want his fingers to brush against me so much I walk to the foot of the stairs and pretend to listen for Max, who has slept through the night since he was three months old.

"How are your folks?"

"My father's all right, re-remarried. My mother died nine years ago," I say. I have considered myself an old orphan, not a heartwarming one, but an orphan nonetheless, ever since.

"I'm sorry. Did it get better between you?"

It got enormously better, as we both saw her death zooming up like the next and necessary exit. We entered her terminal phase like lovers in the shoddiest dime romance: reckless, breathless, selfless, you name it, we threw it out the window. We styled what was left of her blonde hair, and when that was pointless, I spent six hundred dollars I didn't have on a platinum bob and an ash-blonde pixie cut and found myself defending the Gabor sisters against their bad press. We created the River Styx Beauty salon (my mother named it) and made up a gruesome menu of services sought by the decomposing but still-fashionable clients of our high camp owner—"That's M'sieu Styx to you," she'd snap at the other customers, waiting on our side of the bank.

"It got much better." And then I got pregnant and had to miss her all over again, just as if she had been the best mother in the world. "And Gus?"

"Oh, baby. They'll have to drive a stake through his heart."

"That seems fair, for all the heartache he caused us," I say, and then see that I shouldn't have. No matter how old, no matter how bad, we are the only people who can genuinely and expansively bad-mouth our parents. Huddie shakes his head slowly, and I think that I have, with one careless, sincere remark, revealed all my enduring shortcomings.

"You still talk about fair. You've been in this world for forty years and talk about fair. I love that," he says, as if I've shown him my childhood bear collection.

"I like the idea of fair. A little rough justice every now and then is appealing. Unlikely, but appealing."

He tips his head, saluting my idea and me, and I sigh like an old, old woman, because the only choice is kissing or crying over what is behind us and I want to leap ahead without even knowing who he really is or how or if he's leaving June or whether he will really love Max and do we now have to have real holidays instead of my casual improvisations?

I sigh and feel our first time, catching me in the chest. It is still my old stubbly couch and only that beneath my fingertips, but the dark plum silk of his cock unwrinkles in my hand, his flesh hardens, rising up, blindly seeking me. The sweet plump point of his nipple bites my palm. We had no words for our genitals then; we said "this" and "that" and "you" and "me," and when I touched him just the way he wanted, all parts going the right way, his sweat spattering my face, he cried out, "Oh, yes, we're in the zone now." And we laughed so hard we had to stop for a few minutes, but that *is* where we were, and I began to say that too, and kept saying it, with other men, even though it was never as true and saying it brought me closer only to the past and never to the man right next to me. And with no vocabulary at all we had done everything we wanted to do, everything I want to do right now, although in my mind I airbrush us, pulling those young bodies out from our folding fleshy shells, even as I want to see him now, kiss the tender, pitiful changes time has left on that beautiful boy, that handsome young man.

"You could have us both." I think I can say that. "Don't give up what you have." Life will be tolerable (it would have been even better than that if you'd never showed up with those ridiculous flowers and that gigantic car), and once a month it will be all-white gardens drenched in silver moonlight, sweet whole mouthfuls of revelation, a feeling of rightness in the passing essential bits of everyday. And the rest of the time, I will still have the pleasure of being a good mother, even the unmentionable pleasure of being the only parent, the court of first and last resort, the highway, the dead end, and the only gas station for forty miles. And I count on that and Max counts on me, and you are the joker in the deck, my man.

"What are you thinking, Horace?"

"Nothing."

"You lying jellybean."

"You're right. I won't tell you what I'm thinking." And he can't. Pictures of June, tenderly and efficiently pressing her weight on his unbendable leg two hundred times a day until he regained use of his knee; in labor with Larry, her wet face, stunned and determined; Larry as a small boy, tearing through spangled wrapping at Christmas, glitter sticking to his curls; June's appendectomy and most of the choir crowding into her room afterwards, Rosa Grant's flowered straw hat perched on the IV, pink silk ribbons fluttering in front of the vent; six thousand fans, standing for that last basket; June walking the floor with colicky Larry, milk plastering her red chiffon don't-forget-your-husband nightgown to her breasts; flashes of white and black women's bare behinds bouncing in front of him in various motel rooms, their cheeks knotting and opening, the tiny soft arrowhead of hair beneath them; women flipping over in his hands like fresh fish, their breasts swinging and sliding in silky blue-white sacks up to their shoulders, or three shades of brown in sweet handfuls coming to rest on either side of a narrow chest, cocoa pools around purple nipples and stretch marks like the veins of fall leaves, every shape beautiful, calling for his mouth, all of them gone forever.

He smiles. "I'm here. Right here."

"No matter what?"

"Well. That's a lot of ground. Yes, no matter what. No one's going to die from this. And I won't have to shuffle off this mortal coil knowing I lived the wrong life."

He takes my hand. "And what're you thinking? Elizabeth?"

"Nothing."

"You lying hound."

"Yup. And I won't tell you." And I can't: pictures of him trembling over me a million years ago; of Max's face—the first Max—peevish and remorseful in the face of death; the faint, nameless image of my Max's father, blond and tall, foolish but not unkind and not unattractive in his uniform, in bed for twenty-four hours straight until he shipped out, as I hoped he would, and now I watch my son for signs of stupidity and wanderlust; Margaret and Sol reading silently after I'd gone to bed and come out again to see what grown-ups did—"Nothing," my mother said, "we do nothing"; my easy cloistered evenings, doing laundry, making lunch, cutting coupons, playing with Maxie and his Claudette Colbert paper dolls, of which Huddie will surely disapprove, and they will fight and Max will weep and Huddie will turn to dark unreadable stone, and long for the sensible ease of June and the pleasant routine of childless, healthy middle age. And I surely cannot tell him that I'm no more good for me or for him than I ever was, that I will disappoint and confuse him, that I've been alone my whole life, and that it may really be too hard and too late, not even desirable, after such long, familiar cold, to be known, and heard, and seen.

"It's late," I say.
"It's a long drive," he says.

If this were really the end, if this were only my story, I would tell you everything.

ACKNOWLEDGMENTS

I have had the assistance and wisdom of my friends the Reverend Robert Thompson and Nadine Abraham-Thompson, the linguistic help of Josie Zelinka, and the medical insight of Dr. Ron Nudel.

I am grateful to my friend and agent, Phyllis Wender, who knows good from bad and right from wrong and helps me navigate the minefields and mousetraps of the literary world.

I have been lucky in my Random House editor, Kate Medina, a class act, a good captain, and such a mixture of will and savvy that if the act of Creation had been left to her, our world would have been finished in only four days, and with elegance.

My friends and family have provided kind criticism, ungrudging and generous support, and tolerance of all kinds. I am especially grateful to Joy Johannessen, whose supernatural ability to read, see, and understand what is on the page and off has made all the difference.